THE
CASE OF THE
FRENCH
LORD

THE
CASE OF THE
FRENCH
LORD

SANJEEV GANESH

PARTRIDGE
A Penguin Random House Company

To order additional copies of this book, contact
Partridge India
000 800 10062 62
orders.india@partridgepublishing.com

www.partridgepublishing.com/india

Contents

To my parents and my family

Chapter 1

COURT ROOM:

H E SAT ON THE chair. Silent. Gazing at the glass of water, kept a little away from him on the table. He felt a slight tremor while his hands shook. While trying to get a hold of the glass, he spotted his client. 'Sigh!' He was looking depressed. His face showed signs of strain and his hands were shaking. His hair was unkept and his appearance was unlike his usual neat looks.

"Defense, do you have anything else to put forward?" asked the judge. He was fat and sported a bald pate as most judges do. He looked stern and had specs perched on his nose. He kept pushing them up and it kept sliding down his sloping nose.

"At this moment, I don't have any evidence or theories to put forward," he replied back. He continued and added, "The Defense wants some more time to gather up more evidence."

The judge frowned and showed his displeasure. He sat back and thought. *It has already been three months; this cannot continue and must end.*

While he continued to think, the defense and the prosecutor were getting anxious to know what might be the judgement.

The judge then lifted his pen up and started to write his decision. He was feeling worried and kept looking at the convict. After adjusting his coat and his tie, pulling up his specs, took a deep breath and said, "This court, will allow the defense to gather up evidence until the next hearing. If he does not show any, then this court will sentence the convict."

"But sir, this isn't fair. Justice delayed is justice denied, it's already what... 3months." said the prosecutor showing his reproachfulness to the court. "You can't keep extending this, it's an open and shut case." he continued to put forward his views.

The judge seemed to agree with the words of the prosecutor but then he stopped him and said "I know, this cannot continue, but in the next hearing, the court will give its final judgement." Saying this, the judge concluded the hearing, got up and walked away slowly. Everyone could see the frustration and disappointment on the face of the defense. The prosecutor shook hands with his counterpart wishing him well and bid adieu. Slowly, everybody cleared the court premises.

The defense lawyer spotted his client who had a dazed look on his face. Suddenly he remembered that he had promised his client that he would be free again. Since then he had been working day and night gathering up clues and looking for witnesses.

He packed his bag and left the courtroom slowly with heavy burdened heart. He felt tensed and wanted to hurry back home and reassess the case.

The clock struck five in the evening. He felt drained out and kept driving slowly. Adding to his woes the traffic had swelled in massive proportion making his driving jerky. He turned on the radio and tuned into the news channel and heard the warning about an impending storm.

The rain started pouring down heavily as he drove down the street towards his house. He stopped his Honda city and made a dash to the safety of his house. Once safely inside, he made sure that his files were safe and dry.

His house was untidy. It was a single room apartment. He had a small TV, a radio and a battered small steel cupboard where he stacked a few law books and files.

He sat on a wooden chair and turned on the television. He kept pressing the remote aimlessly changing the channels. He then stopped and started watching cartoons. Suddenly the lights went out and in a fit of anger he threw the remote on the bed. His eyes spotted a piece paper peeping from under his files. He looked at it wondering what it could be. He leapt forward and snatched it from under the files.

On seeing the paper he was reminded that the paper was given to him by his client. He also remembered that the paper was given to his client by his uncle when he was dying. Since then he had forgotten about it. He sat on his bed, wore his spectacles and read it.

The secret lies with a cup on the board -13268

It was written in plain black ink and it had an imprint of a flower in the corner of the paper.

He cursed himself for having forgotten all about it.

✼ ✼ ✼

His watch ticked seven in the evening. He sped off to his client's uncle's house. He halted his car at the red light. While waiting, he put his hands inside his bag and took out the piece of paper. He started understanding whatever was written on the paper. Before he could figure it out, the signal turned green and people started honking from behind. He quickly stepped on the accelerator and drove away.

He turned into an alley and stopped his car. He pulled up his sleeves, his Rolex watch read 7:30 late in the evening. He knew he had no time to spare. Thinking so, he made his way into the house.

He entered the house by the keys given by his client. The house was well built. The main door looked very attractive. Inside the house different types of paintings hung and all were very famous, "these paintings would have fetched him a good sum of money" he thought, observing them one after the other. He started looking around for clues.

While looking around, his eyes were drawn towards the sofa. He looked under it and spotted something shiny. He bent down and saw a bunch of keys lying under it. He picked it up and kept it in his bag. "Why would someone hide the keys here?" he thought.

He sat on the sofa and looked at the paper again. He thought of all the possibilities which would solve the puzzle, but it all went in vain. He lifted his head and stared at a cupboard which was positioned exactly in front of him. "Could it be really that simple?" he asked himself.

He stood up and took the keys and tried to open the cupboard. After trying all the keys, the last one opened the cupboard. There were lots of clothes and files inside. He checked every corner of the cupboard when he finally managed to find a locker.

The locker looked simple, but it had a number lock. He needed a combination of numbers to open. He started guessing the combination and understood he needed a five digit number. He thought for a while and looked at the paper again and pressed the numbers written in it. There was silence for some time, then the locker started making noise and slowly the door of the locker opened.

Inside he found a book kept with a small bottle. He wondered why someone would keep a bottle inside a locker. But he knew it had to be of some importance. He took both the book and the bottle and kept it inside his bag. He then closed the locker and left the house.

He returned home and he looked at the clock which showed nine p.m. He sat down on a chair and brought the table lamp closer to the book. He wore his specks and with utmost concentration he opened the book and started going through it.

He had hardly finished a quarter of the book, when he closed it, switched off the table lamp and started shouting "I have got it!"

Chapter 2

4 months earlier.......

"N EXT," SAID THE IMMIGRATION officer. A tall young fellow came forward. He was in blue denim jeans, a striped T-shirt and black cooling glasses. He carried a backpack and a suitcase.

"Passport," demanded the officer.

Having a close look at his watch, he put his hands inside his pocket, took out his passport and slowly placed it on the table. He was constantly looking at his watch and looked anxious. He started to sweat. The officer took the man's passport and started verifying it. "Are you Jimmy?" asked the officer with tilt of his brow.

"Yup! That's me, Jimmy. Owner of the Jimmy export company limited," He replied.

"What do you export?" asked the officer.

"We export canned sardines and tuna" he replied.

"What is the purpose of your visit to India?" asked the officer. Jimmy got more worried.

"My uncle is not well," he stammered.

"Here is your passport, Sir, have a safe and comfortable journey."

"Thank you," he replied back and walked away.

The seats were occupied in the waiting area. But he found a seat and occupied it.

It was 8:30 a.m. sharp when he saw his watch. He checked all his belongings in his backpack, swung it on his shoulder, sped across the gates of the departure and entered into Gate no. 7 and boarded his flight.

$$\text{J}\text{Z} \quad \text{J}\text{Z} \quad \text{J}\text{Z}$$

"Good morning, ladies and gentlemen, this is your Captain speaking. In a few moments, the flight will take off from Colombo airport. The temperature here is slightly above thirty. The duration of the flight is three hours. Please enjoy the flight services. Thank you."

The flight attendants were checking the list of food items and other emergency materials. They were assisting the passengers.

"Good morning, ladies and gentlemen, this is your on board flight attendant. We request everyone to fasten your seat belts, open the window shades and enjoy our on board services. Thank you."

"Excuse me, miss, do you have any eye shades," asked Jimmy, rubbing his eyes.

"I am sorry sir, but the eye shades are out of stock."

Jimmy woke up with a start hearing the flight attendants who were requesting all the passengers to fasten their seat belts again. The plane had started to descend.

"Good afternoon everyone this is your Captain again, thank you for choosing our airline. In a few minutes we shall be landing at the Indira Gandhi international airport. I hope you had a pleasant flight and will choose to fly with us again, thank you."

Jimmy walked off the airport feeling relieved and relaxed. He carried his backpack on his shoulder. He lifted his phone and called his driver as he left the airport.

Outside the airport, lot of people had been standing waiting for their relatives and friends. A few people were standing who were holding placards from various hotels. The outside temperature had a huge difference when compared with the temperature inside.

Jimmy walked out of the airport and started seeing here and there. There he found a man holding a placard reading "Jimmy Connors." He looked a little taller than him. He wore a white shirt with black formal pants and a driver's cap.

Jimmy waved to the man. He walked slowly towards that man and handed over his backpack to him.

He walked towards the parking lot. There the driver directed him to a white cab.

The driver said "Sir, I have orders to take you to the HQ.

He then started the engine, changed the gears, stepped on the accelerator and sped away.

He was conforming that they were not being followed. The driver kept looking at the rear mirror and the side mirror.

Delhi climate felt pleasant, clouds were gathering and the sun was high up in the sky. Suddenly the car stopped outside a big red building looking like a shopping mall. Its outer structure mostly had windows.

The HQ was situated on the outskirts of New Delhi. On the top of the building, the Indian flag was fluttering. The entrance of the HQ was decorated with yellow flowers. Two lion statues carved out of stone stood at the two sides and a statue of a prominent Goddess stood in the middle.

Jimmy entered the HQ and walked straight towards the reception. The lobby was empty. "Hmm probably it is newly built," he thought. When he arrived at the reception there was no one. That surprised him. He waited for some time, looking around the lobby; he saw the furniture new as they were with plastic covering and a tag.

He turned to leave the place. But just then there was a vague buzzing sound. The sound was very loud. It started irritating his ears. He quickly covered his ears to shut out the sound. Suddenly, the noise stopped and there was silence. Then somebody started tapping the mike and spoke "Jimmy Connors? It sounded like a women's voice. There was something in the voice that spread a chill over his body. "Yes," he replied back.

"Take the lift situated right behind you and go to the 5th floor, then take a left and enter the bank.
"Seriously, did I come all the way to get into a bank" he thought. He kept wondering where that sound came from. He kept seeing the room, getting fed up. He walked towards the lift.

❧   ❧   ❧

He walked straight down the corridor and turned left. He saw a big board

YOUR BANK (TRUST US)

He looked at the board and thought that something was fishy. The glass door opened automatically. The bank looked uninhabited with new furniture and computers.
"Hello! He shouted at the top of his voice, is anyone there?

The walls of the bank were painted with attractive textures. He went around the lobby of the bank. He found few boxes placed on a couch. He walked forward, moved the boxes and sat on the chair.

Time seemed to fly but it had been only 5 minutes since he had arrived. He felt tired and his eyes were trying to close down and he wanted to stretch out on the couch and have a good sleep.

Chapter 3

H E FELT SOMETHING VIBRATING and he felt his pocket and found his phone ringing. He slowly put his hands inside his pockets and pulled out his phone.

He wondered who it could be. He kept muttering to himself and the phone continued to ring. "Who could it be?" he asked himself again. He opened the case of his iphone and kept it aside. His phone flashed a private number. He stood up, pressed the talk button and held the phone to his ears.

"Hello?" he spoke. His had a suspicious look on his face. The voice on the phone said, "Behind you there is a door, enter the door, take a seat and press the red button."

"Who are you? What do you want?" But before he could get these answers, the speaker had disconnected the call.

Jimmy looked at his phone closely, trying to figure out the number.

He turned his head and searched for the door. He ran his hand along the wall and felt a protrusion in the wall and applied a slight pressure. Suddenly a door opened on the wall.

He kept his phone inside his pocket and approached the door softly. Jimmy held the knob of the door and then jerked his hands off. "Oh! This is freezing" he thought to himself. His heart suddenly started to race. He held the knob again and turned it clockwise.

"What is this place?" he asked himself. The room was barren. He looked down the floor, he eyes grew bigger. The floor was shiny and well- polished that he could see his reflection. His eyes roamed left to right across the room but the only thing he saw was the shining white floor and the tiles in the wall which were white in appearance. "Oops!" he exclaimed. "I think I have probably entered the wrong room" he thought. "But, I followed all the instructions which were given to me," he said to himself.

Jimmy was still not clear as to what he had to see in the room and what was expected of him. "Is this a cell?" he asked himself. "Am I a prisoner?"

He slowly moved deeper into the room and suddenly he stopped, he turned his head towards the right and then the left and suddenly there …., he stood, with his mouth wide open, looking stunned, then quickly he recovered and was surprised to see a chair. "Hmm, I think my eyes need to be tested."

At the right corner of the room was a chair. Jimmy walked towards the chair. It looked magnificent. The chair had a bright brown leather covering. Moving closer to it he observed the arms of the chair. "Well!, what do we have here, attachments on the arms" he said. On closer observation he saw a belt hanging from the seat.

All of a sudden, he started to think. He lifted his hands and wiped his forehead. "Such a hot day it is today" He said. And suddenly he shouted, "Ah!" he exclaimed. "At last I got it, this might a massaging chair," he said. "I guess. The agency is so caring, they take such good care of their agent like me," he thought.

He sat on the chair slowly, taking off his coat. He folded it neatly and kept it on his lap and relaxed his tired muscles. He fastened the belt tightly and looked around for the red button. There were three buttons red, green and blue.

The phone in his pocket started vibrating and this time, a little louder because silence of the room. He dropped his coat on the white floor and unfastened the belt. His hands moved across into his pockets and picked up the call.

"Press the red button fast as the time is running out."
He sensed the urgency in the voice and blurted out, "Please tell me, who are you?." In his anxiety he forgot about the coat for which he cared very much.

He tried to talk to the caller but the call was abruptly disconnected. Jimmy felt annoyed by the behaviour of the caller. Once again, he buckled up and gently pressed the button. The chair started vibrating and making a mild noise. Jimmy stretched his legs and tried to relax. After a few moments the levels of vibration and the noise started escalating. He realised that the chair was motorised. The chair started to jerk in all possible directions. It was like the chair had a life of its own.

Suddenly the handle of the chair opened and a lever popped out. The top end of the lever was painted red in colour. On both sides of the lever, was painted - ''UP'' and "DOWN," in bold letters.

He was surprised to see the chair with so many attachments. The noise and the vibration of the chair seemed to be a mystery to him. He didn't know what to make of it.

He slowly moved his hands towards the lever and got a firm grip to it. He moved it away from himself. But moving it away didn't seem the right thing to do, because there didn't seem to be any change in the situation of the chair and the lever came back to its original position.

He was surprised to see lever back in its position. So he repeatedly pushed it in the same direction, but it kept coming back. He paused. "I hope I am not leading myself into a trap," he thought, staring at the lever and taking a deep breath, he pulled the lever towards himself.

Suddenly he felt a cold draft. He turned back and suddenly saw the wall of the room open up and a long metal cane with a curved end (which looked more like a walking stick) moving noiselessly towards his chair.

The cane attached itself to the chair. Jimmy felt a little scared when the cane started pulling the chair backwards. When the chair jerked against the wall, he closed his eyes and the vibration started again. Opening an eye, he was astonished to see the floor open apart and an underground corridor opened up which lead down. It seemed bottomless.

A small platform came up slowly and attached itself to the chair. He turned back and saw the cane detach itself and there was silence in the room. Jimmy had a sigh of relief but there still was a gaping hole in the floor. All of a sudden the chair started jerking again. Jimmy's heart started pumping with great speed. His hands sweating and he held on to the handle tightly and by mistake he pressed a button on the right handle of the chair. He felt nervous. His tummy went flip-flop as the chair slowly went down the tunnel and then accelerated to high speed.

※ ※ ※

The chair stopped. Jimmy opened his eyes slowly, his eyes felt heavy. He felt lethargic, slowly; he unstrapped himself and got up. He looked for coat but it was missing. He then he remembered that he had left it in the other room. He saw a door in front of him, opened it gently and entered the room.

The room looked empty. There were files scattered on the desk, the tube light was eerily glowing, there were number of windows.

"Hello! is anybody in here?" asked Jimmy. He looked on and kept his eyes alert.

"Hello! Jack, how are you?" a voice asked. It was a sharp voice.

"Hello, I am fine," he replied immediately vaguely searching for the owner of the voice. He was confused as the caller called him jack. His name was jimmy, but there wasn't a single soul in the room.

Slowly, the chair turned around and a man was seen sitting with his fingers crossed. He wore a brown shirt with a black pant and a vest. His coat was spread out on the back of the chair. As his brown eyes focussed on Jimmy, he sat forward and kept his hands on the desk.

"Have a seat Jack," he said blandly.

Chapter 4

J IMMY MOVED PURPOSEFULLY FORWARD and sat on one of the chairs, alert. The man looked straight into his eyes and then started rearranging the files. Jimmy sat silently, without uttering a single word, looked intently at the man on the other side of the desk. The man looked very much occupied. He kept moving the files up and down as if he was searching for something. "Excuse me? Can I help you?" Jimmy asked after waiting for some time.

The man didn't respond and with a serious expression on his face he continued to rearrange the files. He then picked up a blue file and looked at it. He perched his specs on his nose and looked at Jimmy.

"Jack, welcome back to the agency, here's your next assignment," he said, handing over the file to Jimmy.

"Stop calling me Jack, my name is Jimmy, but who the hell are you?" he said with a stern face.

"Well, I forgot to tell you that I am the new head of this agency and I have given new names to all the agents so that their cover is not blown," he said.

Ok, so.., may I know your name?"

"You can call me Mr. A," he said sitting back on his chair and moving his hands across the table.

"So Mr. A, tell me about my new assignment?" Jimmy asked, He looked happy to be back from vacation. He was eager to know about his new assignment. He had been in the agency for a number of years assisting senior agents.

"Ah! Your new assignment," he exclaimed. He got up and placed his coat gently on the chair and paced around the room.

"Wait," Jimmy said, "what was that chair thing all about?"

"Oh! That's a chair elevator, new technology, sorry for scaring you. Did you like it; it is still in the testing stage." He said.

"You mean you were testing that dangerous thing on me?" he grew angry.

"No, it's not dangerous," he replied. "The elevator is remote controlled, so if you were to fall, then the speed would have decreased automatically."

"And the voice, whose was it?" Jimmy asked.

"Well, that's my personal secretary; she is very interesting. It you meet her, even you would feel the same."

There was silence; both didn't have any conversation for some time.

"Fine," jimmy said, "let's talk, but before that I would like to have some coffee."

"Luckily for you there is a new espresso machine in the HQ." The café was small but it used newer technologies to serve its customers. Jimmy opened A's bag and took out the laptop. He placed it on the table and switched it on.

"Would you like to have something Sir?" asked a waiter after approaching them with a menu card.

"One Espresso please."

"And what about you sir?"

"The same as him," A replied.

"Listen Jack," he said with a serious look on his face, "don't trust anyone on this assignment."

Jimmy nodded his head in assent.

"Have you heard about Jacques Manuel?"

Jimmy nodded; it was like Jimmy knew about him. "That French Lord!" he exclaimed.

"Yes, after making huge profits in France he is planning to establish himself in India."

"You mean drugs…?" Jimmy asked with an astonished look.

"Exactly, drugs, according to our agents, he arrived in Delhi, last Friday and has set the ball rolling."

"Do we have anything about his background," he asked opening a file.

"Well, his parents died when he was very young and since then his uncle had been taking care of him. He was ill-treated there and ran away from his uncle's house." They say that one day, he was found lying in a street, badly injured and unconscious. He was picked up by a government official who was in a very high post. He had taken him home, nursed him back to health and adopted him."

"So, why did he start selling drugs?," he interrupted.

"Just after his graduation from Oxford University, his step father….."

"Wait…, hold on," Jimmy interrupted again. He took his phone out of his pocket placed in silent mode and kept it on the table. "I am sorry, please carry on," he replied again.

"Where was I? Ah yes! his father passed away just after his graduation. After his death, he joined politics, but didn't do well. He started his own business but that too was not successful."

"Then, one day while going through the newspaper he came across an intense article 'Drugs and People' by Miss Jeanne Gaston. It seems that he was highly influenced by the nature of the article." He stopped. "So, there you go," he said leaning back, "this is how he formed the mafia."

"How many people are involved?" Jimmy asked curiously.

"We don't know, there may be more than a hundred. As every day he seems to recruit new people and the people on whom he has lost trust or the people who do suspicious activities are killed."

"Are there any agent who has worked undercover in his setup?" he asked again.

"Yes, the French police had sent two of their best officers but unfortunately they were killed two weeks later."

"Do we have any leads?"

"Well, from our sources we came to know that Jacques met Jeanne a week after the article had been published. So you can start by seeing her, she is in Dubai till Thursday and you have only three days as she travels to Hawaii later that evening."

"Fine, make my travel arrangements and I shall leave immediately." he replied.
"Wait a minute."
"Well, what is it?"
"We are expecting a French agent today. She should have arrived, I believe."

"And how is she going to help us?" Jimmy asked again the expressions on his face changed.

Suddenly there was a rhythmic sound. Jimmy searched his pockets but he didn't find his phone ringing.

Chapter 5

"I THINK IT IS YOUR phone" Jimmy said with a curious look.

Oh! I am sorry," he said. Immediately he moved his hands inside his pocket and answered the call.

"Hello, Yes, speaking ---- yeah --- Hmmm ---ok, send her in when she comes ---yeah----hmmm---ok—thank you."

"What is it?" he asked.

"The French agent is about two miles away from the HQ. We need to get back now, all right," Jimmy said unplugging the charger from the switch. He rolled it and replaced it inside the bag. He then shut the screen of the laptop and placed it in the bag.

ᘓ   ᘓ   ᘓ

Back at the headquarters a room was assigned for the French agent. When Jimmy and his boss went to see the condition of the room they were shocked to see the mess in the room. The room was in a mess, files were scattered on the floor. There was dust and dirt everywhere, spiders and lizards creeping on the walls. "Jimmy go and call the cleaning staff," Mr. A said examining the room

Jimmy agreed and left the room in a jiffy. Moments later Jimmy arrived with a group of people.

"Okay guys we need the room cleaned quickly," Jimmy said, "may I know the name of the agent." He asked Mr. A, but for some reason, he ignored him. "Excuse me sir, I probably asked you something," his tone raising. But no answer, he kept arranging a few files.

Jimmy started to feel annoyed. He asked him again but there was no reply. Suddenly his phone vibrated. Jimmy looked on, his boss moving away from the files and received the call at the corner of the room.

"Hello----yes---great!—send her inside—through the stairs" and he disconnected the phone. He kept his phone back in his pockets and walked towards the door. His coat was covered with dust. "Stay here, I am going to freshen up, I have asked an official to bring the agent and then you are off to Dubai."

"OK," Jimmy said and managed a smile. He left the room and leaving the door half open. Jimmy started looking around the room, opening files and a few documents and there he found a file.

The file looked shabby, and contained some old papers. At the bottom of the file, it read 2007. Jimmy thought for a while and then opened the file. There was silence again. He kept verifying the papers when suddenly he stood still looking stunned.

꒰ꫝ꒱   ꒰ꫝ꒱   ꒰ꫝ꒱

A tall slim woman came through the entrance and walked through the lounge. She had long waist length hair, coloured brown; she had blue eyes, with a broad chin and smooth cheeks. She wore black jeans and red T shirt which was covered with a jacket.

She smiled as she saw an official approaching her with extended hands. They shook hands and introduced themselves.

"*Bon après midi*, agent Catherine," said the official. "Arrangements will be made for the luggage to be sent to the hotel." He escorted her to Mr. A's chamber " T h a n k you," she replied.

She entered the chamber after a courtesy knock. She saluted smartly to Mr. A.

On enquiring briefly on her journey, Mr. A directly started talking about the case.

"I am sure you can help us a lot in this case," the boss said shaking hands with her. "I am honoured to be helping you and I think you must have got the necessary details from the French embassy," she said.

He looked at her blankly, saying nothing, and then as if coming out of a daze he gave a jerk and said, "Yes, we had received it, but we have to wait for a reply as it has gone to the Chairman. After he approves it, then we will do the needful."

Catherine switched on her mobile and immediately put it back in her pockets. "Agent, for this mission, you will need a partner and he is waiting for you on the 5th floor, use the stairs as the lift isn't working."

"Yes boss," she replied and walked out of the room towards the lobby. She looked around the lobby but she couldn't find the staircase. She turned back and saw no one, it was an eerie feeling as the lobby and the entrance was empty.

Moments passed and she stood there like a statue but alert. Slowly moving only her head and trying to sight the stairs. But alas! She didn't find them. She thought she would try the lift and walked towards it and stood there. She felt apprehensive as she pressed the button of the lift.

There was a loud clanging noise for a few minutes and suddenly, beside the lift, the wall opened up like a garage shutter and there lo! It was there – the staircase, painted brownish red. She stared at it amazed and then she started climbing up.

When she kept her foot on the first step, there was the noise again and her heart started a rhythmic thump which matched the noise around. It had stopped again and then suddenly the handles of the staircase started to move. "What is this," she murmured to herself. She was curious to know what it was and then suddenly the staircase also started to move up. "Escalator," she said to herself. She stood on the first step and the escalator flattened itself and looked more like a slide. It started winding itself smoothly around the pillar. She looked astonished as she moved up. She had not seen anything like this before.

She was still in a daze as she took the ride on the escalator. The escalator turned left and right and finally it turned into a walkway.

"Is that a door?" she said, spotting the door at a distance.

As she approached the door, she saw a light flicker at regular intervals as if giving some sort of a signal. As she stood in front of the door she spotted a small digital screen with a smiley.

♫ ♫ ♫

Jimmy was still seeing the file, his eyes were growing bigger. He was trying to remember something which he had forgotten. "I have seen him somewhere," he said looking at the file and took a look at cupboard.

Suddenly, the whole cupboard started to move. Jimmy looked on. He hid the file immediately. A tall woman walked side the room and there both stood looking stunned. They had a close look at each other.

"Brother?" she asked him, her backpack slipping off her shoulders. "What are you doing here?" she asked him again. She still looked at him with a stern face totally confused.

"Don't tell me, you are the French agent," he said, with a slanting face. He was still confused of all the things which had happened since his arrival at the HQ. "Yes, I am. Don't you tell me that you're my partner"?

Behind Jimmy the wooden door and Mr A entered the room holding an envelope. "Ah! Agents, well, here are you tickets, and your flight is scheduled in another 5 hours. Any questions?"

"Yes," Jimmy said, "you collected my bio-data before I joined the agency, right?" He looked at Jimmy and gave him an obvious look on his face and replied, "Yes, we did."

"Then, didn't you know that this agent is my sister and I hate her," he agreed with Jimmy and walked away from the room. But then he peeped from outside and said, "well it's been almost about 8 years since you worked, so we thought you would be happy to work with her again."

"Why should you hate me," she said. "Don't you remember it was because of you, he escaped," she added.

"It wasn't because me," Jimmy replied raising his tone. "It was you, you said your plans always work, and then what happened, he escaped."

The voice from a microphone crackled, "Your car is ready for airport."

Hearing the voice, the argument stopped. Both of them looked around to locate the microphone.

"Ok, we are starting," he said.

He looked at Catherine and hugged her. "I am sorry for the argument, let's go. We have something important to do," he said with a bold voice.

"That's some encouraging words," she replied and slowly they left the room.

♫   ♫   ♫

Chapter 6

A FTER COMFORTABLY HAVING A seat, Catherine put her hands in her pocket and picked up her phone. She opened the case and started working on it. She was busy gathering up information about a dead person at the same time she could hear the announcements which were being made regarding the arrival and departure of flights.

Meanwhile, Jimmy, who had a seat beside Catherine, was working on his IPhone when suddenly he opened his bag and started to search for something. He looked for it and lifted it. Catherine saw him taking out an old shabby file. "What is this file," she asked. "Not now Cath," he said immediately, "I will tell you later."

Catherine looked at the file and then looked at Jimmy. He looked serious about the file. He closed it and went into a deep thought. Even after repeated prodding from Catherine, Jimmy refused and started ignoring her.

✧   ✧   ✧

After the Emirates flight took off from runway 2 at exactly 04:30 in the evening, it was ascending at the normal velocity and reached altitude of 35000 ft. at no time. As soon as it straightened and moved towards Mumbai. Jimmy opened his bag and pulled out that file again. Catherine gave a look at him and kept her phone inside.

"Jimmy, can't you tell me what this is?" she asked for one last time. "Not now," he said again with an irritating voice. He opened the file and pulled out a small notebook form his bag and started to write down. Catherine observed all this, saying nothing. She was growing curious. She closed the window shade and in a fraction of second she pulled the file and kept it with her.

"Cath, give the file back," he said. "First you tell me what is going on." "I told you not now," he replied. "Now or no file," she said immediately. "Fine," he shouted exasperatedly.

All the other passengers looked at Jimmy. They murmured to each other. The air hostess walked towards Jimmy. Before she could talk something, Jimmy apologised and gave her an innocent look. She left immediately with a big smile on her face.

"You want to know what's in this file, right." Catherine nodded her head. She was happy that she could get to know what it is. She tilted partially towards Jimmy and waited eagerly for Jimmy to explain what was going on.

"Excuse me, Sir, would you like to have a drink?" the air hostess asked Jimmy. She was fair, had black curly hair on which she wore a head band which was pink in colour and had flower petals in it.

"Yes, a red wine," he responded with a smile. "You drink," Catherine asked. She looked surprised. As she watched the hostess, pour the wine in the glass, "Yeah! Sometimes," he replied. Jimmy held the glass and gulped it down. "Give me more," he demanded and the hostess topped his glass before going to attend the other passengers.

Meanwhile, Catherine was enjoying the lovely view over the clouds through the window. She went down the memory lane remembering the time spent with Jimmy and the adventures with him 8 years ago. Then she suddenly turned her head and focussed on the file. She slowly opened it and started going through the file.

She kept turning the pages and then stopped. She saw a photo and started thinking. "I think, I have seen her somewhere," she thought. She turned her head towards Jimmy and found him drinking the wine. He put down the glass and then dosed away to sleep.

"Jim, wake up," Catherine said but he did not wake up. Inching closer to Jimmy, Catherine pulled out the note pad in which Jimmy was writing and also took out his cell phone. She gently pulled out the table from the seat before her and placed the things on it. She took his phone and opened its casing.

What she saw next was that, head phones sprung out and the phone automatically switched itself on. She raised it in the air and noticed words flashing from it as the head phones dangled. 'Wear the head phones' it flashed. Without giving it a thought she wore the head phones. Seconds after wearing it the phone turned blank. She kept touching the screen but it didn't show any change. Moments passed but the phone was still blank. Just as she was going to remove the headphones, a play button displayed on the screen. Suddenly the air hostess stopped by and picked up the wine glass, the bottle and she left.

Her focus went back on Jim's phone. She still wore the headphones. Her fingers clicked the centre of the screen and then sat back unbuckling herself from the seat. The phone went blank again and then a visual of Jimmy appeared.

"Cath, Listen," Jimmy said. "This MMS will be destroyed after it gets over. So listen carefully."

Catherine quickly opened the note pad and got ready to write. She was looking nervous but she was excited to know what was going to come next.

"Eight years ago, on our first mission at the Hadley school, after Clarke's escape, he joined Manuel and ran few storage houses at Nice. But then he suddenly disappeared. He was a trusted and a loyal friend of Manuel. Inside the blue file, there is a clipping of the '*Le Figare*' which says that Manuel died in a blast on 20th of February, 2009."

Catherine listened to whatever the video said and kept writing down the important notes of Jimmy. Beside her Jimmy murmured in his sleep but he continued to doze.

Mr. A gave me a new assignment to catch Manuel. But before you entered the room to see me, I found a yellow file which had details about Clarke stating that he visited a hospital in Dubai on 11th Feb and Manuel attended a party on the 22nd Feb." Suddenly the phone went blank again apparently the MMS got destroyed.

Catherine sat there, looking down at the notes which she had written; she held the paper and slowly tore it from the pad. She took a new page and with a neat handwriting she rewrote her notes. She turned sideways and saw Jimmy rubbing his eyes.

Jimmy woke up with a start after rubbing his eyes. He saw Catherine sitting down with his phone and the files. "Why didn't you tell me about Clarke," she asked furiously.

"I just wanted to be sure."

Chapter 7

J IMMY FELT SOMETHING WAS not right. He knew the red wine had been drugged which has made him dozy. Even after he woke up he did not feel right. His head was dizzy and was trying to reorient himself.

Suddenly Catherine was standing beside Jimmy and was waiting for him to move to get back to her seat. "Where were you?" Jimmy asked and looked at the things and gadgets kept on the table.

"I was in the lavatory," she replied. "Which hospital in Dubai did he visit?," she asked Jimmy immediately. "I don't know," he responded.

"So what's next?"

"When we reach Dubai, I will send a copy of this yellow file through my phone to the headquarters and they will let us know," Jimmy said. He was feeling excited about this, but, at the same time he was thinking of some old memories.

"Isn't the hospital's name written in the file?"

"Yes, it is written but we need to be absolutely sure, because we have to report our findings to the HQ."

Just then the plane made a sudden jerk and descended. "Ladies and gentlemen," the pilot said, "in a few minutes we will land in terminal 3 of Dubai International airport. At present the temperature in Dubai is just over 19 degrees Celsius. Please put back the tables, fasten your seat belts."

Catherine started to pack up the things and buckled herself. She was really excited. She was looking out of the window towards the sunset. She hadn't seen such a lovely and bright sunset in her whole life.

♫   ♫   ♫

"Dubai International airport, the major airline hub of the middle east," said the pilot as he was speaking the special features of Dubai. The plane made a smooth touch on the ground. Passengers could see the terminal 3 of the airport.

Jimmy peeped out of the window and saw the big structure made of glass. The plane moved at a slow speed and ultimately docked at the centre of the terminal. Immediately, the ground force deployed the chute and the people started to move out of the plane.

♫   ♫   ♫

The plane was empty and all the passengers had disembarked. The ground force had been cleaning up and the airhostesses were getting things ready for their next shift. One of the airhostesses was moving across the deck. She was checking if anything was missed out during the cleaning. As she neared the lavatory, she was informed, the lavatory was not cleaned. I'll check it," she said. She entered the lavatory.

She first tilted the dustbin and started throwing the tissues and bits of papers. As she was doing so, she found a paper, crushed. "This is it," she murmured. She picked it up and made it straight. Moments later she crushed it again and put it in the bag. She made a swift exit from the lavatory and informed the ground force official to continue with the cleaning and sat down on a seat. She picked her phone and dialled a number.

"Hello boss?" she said with a low tone.
"What is it," he asked.
"The two agents know your identity. They know you are not Manuel. They will get to know who you really are. What's your next move?"

He disconnected the phone abruptly. She was shaken. She got up from the seat and continued to do her job. Suddenly passengers entered the plane and she started welcoming them. "My next shift," she thought and forgetting everything she got back to her daily routine.

♫   ♫   ♫

Jimmy walked straight down the escalator after his immigration check, with him, Catherine, holding her purse in her hands. Jimmy was growing impatient. He wanted to send his findings immediately to the HQ. As they reached the basement, Jimmy and Catherine took up seats in the waiting area.

Catherine handed her phone to Jimmy and he opened the file and kept on clicking up pictures and covered the whole file. He then quickly sent it as an email to HQ.

"Hello, Mr. A."

"Yes," he responded. "I am sending pictures to your email. This is very important."
"I'm on it," he replied and disconnected the call.

Jimmy wanted to relax but Catherine got up and pulled Jimmy's hand. "What are you doing?" Jimmy asked. He looked tired and his eyes were drooping. "Come on, get up, we have lots of work to do," she said.

Jimmy made a slow exit, He saw a man holding a white board saying "Jack." "Let's go," he said to the man, his head dizzy. "Sir, are you okay?" the man asked. Suddenly Catherine came in between and said, "He's not well."

Both of them sat in the car and the driver drove away. He turned left and then right and drove straight ahead. "Look at that Jim," Catherine said looking towards the west." "That's the World Trade Centre," she said. "Nice, big," he said and drifted off to deep sleep. His head moved and then Catherine pushed him towards the window.

ॐ ॐ ॐ

Fisher entered an old mill in southern Mumbai. He wore blue jeans and white shirt with leather jacket. He took out his gun and walked inside. People were standing in their respective positions with snipers.

A man was seated in a wooden chair and Fisher approached him. He saw only his back and looked at the other guards.

"Boss, did you call me," he asked him.
"Yes, take some men and kill these agents in Dubai before they meet anyone. If you fail we will be in grave danger of getting busted by these people," he said and handed over the photos of Jimmy and Catherine.

"Yes boss, it will be done immediately. Their first stop will be the hospital. I will send our men to kill them there."
"Fine, after you finish the job, you will be properly rewarded."
"Thanks boss," he said, feeling rejoiced and left the place. After coming out from the mill, Fisher took out his phone and made a call.

"Hello, listen, send some men to Dubai. I need them to do a job for me." I shall send the description of the job."

♫ ♫ ♫

Catherine's phone was ringing. She remembered giving it to Jimmy and she retrieved it from his pocket. He was in a deep sleep on the couch. Catherine picked up the call.

"Hello?"
"Agent, it's me," said Mr. A.

"Yes sir," Catherine replied.

"I have got the picture and the hospital is 15 minutes east to Burj Khalifa. The name is Dubai City Hospital. You will meet a Dr. Mohamadden Rehman, chief doctor of the hospital."

"And what about Jeanne?" she asked.

"She is still in Dubai and will be leaving 2 days later. You have lots of time. She is having a conference at Burj Khalifa."

"Ok sir, I get it. Thanks."

Chapter 8

T HE LIGHTS REFLECTED ON the water fountain beside the Burj Khalifa. Jimmy was observing the water fountain and wiped his face clear from the sprinkles. He moved away from the fountain and walked straight ahead towards the entrance. On entering the building he looked around admiring the decorations which were present in the lobby. His phone started beeping.

"Hello."

"Mr. Jimmy, Ms. Jeanne is free. You can see her at Atmosphere Lounge."

Jimmy disconnected and went directly to the reception. A man was seated in a chair at the reception in his uniform. He was working on his computer when Jimmy stopped by.

"How can I help you sir?" the man asked him politely.

"I want to know where the Lounge is." Jimmy asked.

"Take the lift and go up 122nd floor." Jimmy thanked him and sped to the nearest elevator.

❧   ❧   ❧

The man at the reception watched Jimmy going inside the elevator. As soon as the elevator closed its doors, the man picked up his phone and made a call.

"Hello, it's me, he is going up the elevator" and immediately disconnected the phone and quickly got back to work.

♫ ♫ ♫

Catherine was looking around the corridors of the hospital. Nurses and some patients were moving around. She reached the end of the corridor, moved right and then she stopped in front of a room. It had a glass door for its entrance. In the centre of the door, was a name board in black. It had the name- 'Mohamadden Rehman – Chief Doctor'.

She knocked the door and opened it. "Excuse me sir?" she said and entered the room. She looked around and saw him working on a file. He took a quick glance at Catherine and asked her to come in and have a seat.

"Sir, my name is Catherine. I am writing an article on plastic surgeons. I want to ask about some of the risky cases that you have attended to."

"Just a minute," he said and kept away his file. He removed his specs and opened his drawer from which he picked out a file and riffled through it and picked out a photo and showed it to her.

She was surprised to see that the photo was Clarke's, but she kept her face devoid of any expression and looked enquiringly at the doctor to continue.

"This man came to me two days before the French lord died and asked me to recreate his face and put Manuel's face on him."

"Didn't you tell him something," she asked making notes on her notepad.

"I told him that it's a difficult operation as his right side of the face was badly damaged but he threatened me with dire consequences."

"And anything else."

"He called me up a month later and said his life is in danger and wanted me to do a plastic surgery again. But I refused."

"And then."

"He never rang me up. But somebody called on his behalf."

"Can I have the name of this somebody," she asked.

Dr Rehman was handing over a piece of paper to Catherine and when a man abruptly entered with a bag. Dr Rehman and the man looked at each other and suddenly he stood up. Catherine kept her notepad inside and had a close look at the man. When he put his hands inside the bag as though searching for something, Catherine felt something amiss and the doctor stood still.

The doctor and the man started talking in Arabic. Catherine stood up and started to leave when the man pulled out a revolver and fired three bullets which hit Rehman on his chest and he collapsed to the ground immediately.

Catherine turned around shocked, and she saw the doctor lying on the ground. Before she could reach for the gun, the man turned towards her and said, "You are next," aiming at her.

❧   ❧   ❧

Fisher went back into the mill. He had a big smile on his face; all the guards were in the same position as he had seen them before. He walked a little faster this time but when he reached the wooden chair, he could not find his boss. He looked around but he only saw the guards. Just then a hand moved forward and it rested on Fisher's shoulder. When Fisher slowly turned back he saw his boss, holding a cup of coffee. "Boss, good news. They have been captured," Fisher said with lots of excitement.

"That's great, but now, you fly to Paris. In my house there is a file about our finances, which I want."

"Ok boss, I will leave tomorrow morning," he responded and left the place.

❧   ❧   ❧

Jimmy was still seated in the lift and it was still moving. It had reached the 90th floor when suddenly his phone rang.

"Hello – Hi Cath, what did the doctor say?"

"Listen, where are you?" she asked.

"I'm at Burj. Is everything all right? You sound tensed and nervous?"

"A man entered the room and killed the doctor. I somehow escaped. Be careful, they might be following you."

But before Jimmy could reply, Catherine hung up. He replaced his phone in his pocket and started feeling tensed. He opened his bag and looked inside. While moving the things inside, he found his notepad.

Minutes passed and the lift slowed down and it stopped at floor no. 122, the Lounge. He got off the lift and he entered through a glass door in front of the lift.

The Atmosphere Restaurant was divided into four parts – lounge, restaurant, bar and a grill restaurant. Jimmy walked straight ahead into the Lounge and zipped back his bag. When he lifted his head again, beside the central window, a lady was seated with a glass of red wine in her hand. Jimmy moved forward quickly and approached her. He took a few minutes to look out of the window and observed the beautiful sight. He spotted the desert from a distance

"Are you Ms. Jeanne Gaston?" Jimmy asked. She placed her glass down and nodded and looked at him enquiringly

"Good evening, I am Jimmy" he said and asked her if he could join her. She gestured him to sit down.

Jimmy occupied the chair and made himself comfortable.

"Why do you want to meet me?" she asked

"Sorry to bother you, let me come straight to the point, I want to know about my uncle, Jacques Manuel."

"I don't want to talk about him," she said at once and started to leave.

"Wait, please don't go. My aunt has been anxiously waiting for three years, but he has not returned. His friend said he had met you." She looked at Jimmy and slowly sat back at her seat.

"Yes, it's true. He called me and we met at my house. A year later he accused me of a murder and I had to run away from France. My friend called me up a week later saying that Manuel occupied my house and is living there."

"Can I get your house address"?

"14, *Rue de plante*, 95100, *Argenteuil, Paris.* Jimmy quickly noted it down and kept his note pad inside.

"*Merci*," Jimmy said picking up his bag and got up from his place when Jeanne suddenly collapsed. Jimmy ran back and looked at her. The red wine was split on the floor. Jimmy held her hand and checked her pulse. "Dropping," he said and finally it stopped. She lay on the floor.

"Call the ambulance," he shouted.

He felt a hand on his shoulders and when he turned around; he saw a man in black jeans and leather. "Sir, I am an agent. I have information from the agency," he said and immediately Jimmy walked away with the man. They waited for the lift and got into the lift.

"What is it that you want to tell me?," Jimmy asked looking for his note pad.

"Your fellow agent has gathered up clues and is going out of Dubai.

"Very well, thank you," Jimmy replied and pulled out his phone. He was dialling a phone number when the man knocked him down.

Chapter 9

"**M**R. A, IT'S ME Catherine. I am at the Burj to pick Jimmy but he is not picking up my call."

"Fine, you get in and ask somebody and call me back." He cut the phone.

Catherine looked worried. Jimmy had not picked up her call since an hour but yet any response from his side. Catherine walked swiftly searching for the reception table.

"Excuse me, she said to a busy lady at the reception. "Yes ma'am, how can I help you?"

"Did a person come here asking for the Lounge?"

"Yes ma'am, he was taken away to hospital an hour ago."

"Which hospital?" Catherine asked her heart racing and pumping.

"I don't know."

Ok thanks," she said and started to leave when the receptionist intercepted and looked for something in the desk.

"Here, that man dropped this from his pocket," the lady reached out to Catherine's hands and handed over a note pad. Catherine thanked the receptionist and walked back towards the exit.

At the parking area, Catherine pulled out her phone and pressed the call button.

"Hello, Mr. A, it's me Catherine. Jimmy fainted in the Lounge and was taken to a hospital but I don't know which one."

"Fine, there is an agent in Dubai who is on a holiday. I will tell him to look him up. Move quickly to the airport. Go to the airport reception and collect your ticket and pass.

⁊ ⁊ ⁊

Fisher was waiting patiently for the boarding call of his flight. Time ticked past one O'clock early morning. He lifted his brown bag and placed his bag on his lap.

He noticed his phone sing the caller tune.

Fisher opening his bag picked up his phone and answered a call.

"Hello, boss," answered a man quickly.

"Yes," Fisher replied.

"Jimmy is with me. I am bringing him to the Paris house."

"Great, well done, I am sure boss will give you a good reward," saying so Fisher cut the line and relaxed in the chair.

⚜ ⚜ ⚜

Catherine was going through Jimmy's note pad while the air hostesses were serving food. The plane was flying high above the clouds and the sun shined bright at her face. She closed the window shades and continued to assess the note.

She was worried and was constantly thinking about Jimmy. The air hostess had finished serving food. When Catherine tore another page from the note pad and wrote another note to confirm her understandings.

When she had finished writing, she was astonished to see her writings. "So, it is true that Manuel was replaced by Clarke," she murmured, "but the only question is why?"

⚜ ⚜ ⚜

Charles de Gaulle airport was known as the finest airports in France. It was the time of dawn. Air France flight coming from Dubai landed at Terminal 3 of the airport. Catherine hurriedly packed her bag and ran down the stairs and boarded a bus to get to the main arrival section.

Moments passed and Catherine was seated in the bus. She was trying to ring Jimmy's phone but there was no answer. She called Mr. A immediately.

"Hello, he asked sipping a mug of coffee on his couch.

"Hello, Mr. A, it's me Catherine."

"Catherine, did you find Jimmy," he asked her hurriedly placing his coffee mug on the table.

"NO, I didn't find him at the airport, any progress from your side?."

"The agent had searched every hospital in Dubai but his efforts went in vain."

"Ok sir, I am at Paris. I am going to Manuel's house in Argenteuil."

"Good work Catherine, The agent in Dubai is trying his level best to find Jimmy."

✦ ✦ ✦

Jimmy was having nightmares. He was sitting in a chair, his hands and legs were tied up with a rope. People were around him, each holding a pistol and suddenly he woke up. His shirt was drenched in sweat. He was tied to a chair even in reality. He was feeling tired. He was vigorously moving the chair trying to untie himself.

Suddenly, the door in front of him opened wide and a man entered. Jimmy could recognise him. It was the same man who had tricked him in the lift and knocked him out.

"Where am I?" Jimmy asked furiously.

"You are at Manuel's house in Paris," he replied holding a glass of water in his hands. "Boss asked me to take you hostage and that's what I did," he added.

"You are doing a big mistake."

"Shut up," the man said holding Jimmy's lower jaw and forcing him to open his mouth and drink the water.

After having a gulp of water, Jimmy's head was becoming heavy and then he dosed off asleep.

Fisher was aboard another Air France flight which was bound from Mumbai to Paris. The plane was just 20 minutes away from landing at Charles de Gaulle. Beside him two of his seats were empty and he was comforting himself at the window seat.

He was gazing out of the window at the clouds. When the plane came down the clouds and there was the ground. While having a beautiful aerial view, an airhostess suddenly stopped by him and sat in the seat beside Fisher and whispered urgently.

"Listen, Catherine is in Paris and Jimmy is in the house held captive," she said.

"Anything else?" Fisher asked.

"Yeah, when you go back to Mumbai, you have to meet a man called Naresh. He is Catherine's uncle but he works for us. He has some financial information on the trade," she said.

Fisher thanked her for the information and he turned again to view the land. She sat there for a while looking relaxed. She took a deep breath and slowly pushed up her watch and moved closer towards Fisher.

Suddenly, the pilot was requesting all the crew for landing when she moved closer to Fisher. He was enjoying the aerial view and then without having a thought the airhostess moved her and head and kissed Fisher, murmured something to him and walked away.

Fisher kept looking at her. He rubbed his cheeks and had a great smile on his face. After landing, when all the passengers were leaving, Fisher was very happy. He walked with the line and beside the lavatory he met the air hostess and murmured to her which made her blush and Fisher got off the plane.

Chapter 10

CATHERINE STOOD STILL. ARMED with a gun, the morning sun was making way to come up the sky at the horizon. She moved stealthy across the porch and slowly crawled over the wet grass and hid behind a mango tree. She ignored the

She was just about to go behind the house, when her phone started to vibrate.

She ignored the call for a while but then, she picked up the call, managing to hide behind the tree.

"It's me, A, where are you?"

"At Manuel's house."

"Whatever you want from there, take and leave because Fisher is going to arrive there and he is very dangerous. If possible, kill him."

"You got it boss," she replied and threw her phone in the bag and zipped it. She glanced at the window and swiftly moved away from the tree and stood beside the front wall. She knelt down and crawled under the window and rolled towards the entrance of the backyard of the house.

Butterflies fluttered over the grass and sunflowers were dancing at the morning sunlight. Catherine peeped inside the house, but there wasn't anyone seen. She crawled slowly and spotted a pale yellow door.

She turned the knob of the door and entered the house. There was an old shelf with different types of buckets while moving in. She noticed ropes around a chair. She knew someone had kept here. She continued to observe the room when she saw another room. She slowly edged towards it, the door suddenly opened. And a man stood in front of Catherine holding a gun, his hair frizzed up and his shirt dirty and wet-- and he was.......

"Jimmy?" Catherine said.

"Hi Cath," he replied putting down his gun. Catherine walked swiftly and gave Jim a big hug.

Moments passed and both of them were back to normal. Catherine was constantly asking him of how he got there but Jimmy refused to answer because he didn't know it himself. Suddenly a man entered the room and aimed his pistol at Jimmy.
"Very good reunion and a full pot of reward for me," he said. Catherine held Jimmy's hands; her mind was thinking of plans get them both out of this. Just then, the front door opened and the man turned to see who it was. Jimmy quickly grabbed his gun and immediately shot him in the stomach. He fell down with a thud hitting his head on the wall and sank on the floor and lay still.

Catherine moved across to check on the visitor who was at the door. As she moved, she saw files and pieces of paper lying in stacks beside the door. When she arrived near the main entrance, she spotted a tall man standing beside the door holding a small suitcase looking around.

Catherine's phone vibrated, but she had dropped in the store room. Jimmy picked it up and answered the call.

"Hello?" Jimmy asked.

"Jimmy, thank God, you are okay," Mr. A said.

"Boss, I am fine."

"I am sending a picture of Fisher to you. He is in Paris."

"Fine Boss," Jimmy said and disconnected the call. Seconds later, the phone vibrated again when Jimmy switched on the phone, he had received the picture of Fisher, having a quick look at the picture. Jimmy moved out of the room and walked towards Catherine. When he was about to approach Catherine Jimmy was stunned to see the man with the suitcase.

"Fisher?" asked Jimmy.

"Yes," Fisher replied.

All the three of them stood still. There was silence in the room. Suddenly, Fisher dropped his suitcase and removed his gun.

"Ah! The two Indian agents trying to stop Manuel," he said holding his gun towards Catherine.

"Listen," Catherine said trying to negotiate with Fisher, "Manuel is dead and we have proof."

"What nonsense," he ordered me to bring a file."

"We have proof, we can show it you."

"Forget the proof, I don't want it, but now let me get this file, then you guys are dead."

Fisher went silent. He was looking around for the file. Suddenly a woman appeared at the doorstep. She was dressed in an air hostess uniform. Fisher quickly hid his gun and went forward to meet her.

"Honey, who are these people," she asked closing the front door. Fisher was worried he held her hand said, "Dear, meet my two old friends. I was with them in school. This is Jimmy and this is Catherine."

Jimmy and Catherine both had a warm hand shake with the lady.

"Now sweetheart," Fisher said, "you go upstairs and make yourself fresh and I will join you." Catherine was observing her dress and found her name tag which read 'Alisha. She went upstairs.

"Right now your death is cancelled. I need to find that file and then you are gone. I let you free," Fisher said searching for the file in a rack. Jimmy looked at his gun which he had hidden it in the rack.

Catherine moved forward and said "why did you do all this?"

"Because I am being forced to. If I don't then she gets killed."

"Can't you just leave him saying you are not well," Jimmy interrupted.

"A year ago, my best friend fell in love with a girl, he used the same excuse and when it was found that he lied, he was killed."

Time passed and Fisher was still searching for the file. Catherine and Jimmy were looking at different file kept and going through the things done by Manuel.

While going through the last rack, Jimmy found a new file. It seemed like it was never used. He handed over the file to Fisher. Catherine was still looking around the racks when she heard footsteps as it someone was walking down the stairs. Catherine saw Alisha and there she was looking beautiful.

"This is it; this was the file that I was looking for. Thanks Jim."

"Jimmy quickly pulled out the gun from the rack and aimed at Fisher. Catherine was shocked. Alisha gave a big scream.

"Enough," said Jimmy, "you first sent a man to kill us and now you are letting us free. I know it. This is a big trap in which you want to kill us."

"It's not like that," Fisher replied.

"Shut up, it is like that. Cath, take the file," Jimmy said. His angry face scared Catherine. Alisha was requesting Jimmy to put down the gun but he did not listen to her.

After shouting so many times, Catherine pulled the file from Fisher. Even he was scared. He started to move backwards but Jimmy noticed it.

"Jim, what are you doing," Catherine said clutching the file away. Jimmy did not respond to her too.

"Any last words Fisher,"

"No, you can go ahead and shoot me."

"No…." Alisha shouted.

Jimmy quickly got a good aim and without thinking pulled the trigger.

Fisher collapsed. Alisha was stunned. She broke out. Catherine was surprised and looked at Jimmy.

"How could you do this Jim?" Catherine asked. But Jimmy picked up the file and pulled Catherine out of the house.

Chapter 11

8 hours later …………..in Mumbai

J IMMY AND CATHERINE WERE seated in a car. Catherine was still angry at him for shooting at Fisher. She could still remember how Alisha had broken down.

"For one last time Jim," she said, "why did you kill him?'. Jimmy was irritated. He didn't want to answer but Catherine kept asking him the same question.

"Okay, Fisher didn't die."

"Don't lie; you shot him in front of me."

"Listen," he said whispering in her ears and kept talking to her. When he finished, the car stopped and the driver turned back.

"Sir, we have reached Trident."

"Okay, thank you, here's your money," he said handing over three hundred rupee notes.

After checking in the hotel, they were moving up the lift. Catherine held Jimmy's hand and said "I apologise for being angry at you."

"Ok that's fine," he said.

When the lift opened, his phone started ringing. He got off the lift and picked up the call.

"Hello----Mr. A, now what------Chennai ----- the pit ----- okay, fine I'll go there, but what should I get?" But he didn't reply to that question and cut the line.

"So," Catherine said, "What the plan now."

"You are going to meet uncle Naresh," Jimmy said while Catherine was trying to open the door. "And what about you, Jim?"

"I am going to Chennai to get something."

After Catherine placed her luggage at the corner of the room, Jimmy waved his hands and left the room with his luggage. Catherine locked the room and went into the bathroom for a shower.

Minutes later, while Catherine had finished her bath, she was dressing up when the main door suddenly opened. She heard the noise of the main door. After dressing herself, she moved out of the bathroom holding a gun.

She walked and turned suddenly. Aiming the gun at the person and then dropped it down. "Whoa Cath, easy down," said Jimmy, placing the room key at the table. "You seriously gave me a scare," he said.

"What did you forget Jim?"

"Oh!" He Exclaimed, "nothing much. I forgot to give you the address of Uncle Naresh.

He extended his hands and gave Catherine a piece of paper and left the room.

Catherine picked up her gun and put it in her backpack. She threw the towel on the bed and picked her comb from her bag and stood in front of the mirror and combed her hair.

Moments later, Catherine was ready. She tied her hair, hung her bag and left the room with an intent look on her face.

♫ ♫ ♫

Manuel was frustrated and worried. The last call he had got from Fisher was when he had boarded the flight to Paris. As time passed, he worried more. He was sitting in his old chair which had a red leather cushion.

He saw his men patrol the mill and from the windows too. He saw his men with arms. He grew angry and suddenly he got up. "Commander," he shouted at the top of his voice. "Yes boss," he said holding a revolver in his hands.

"Bring me the traitor fast and get me my gun."

"Right away sir," he responded and left the plane running to get the traitor.

Manuel was walking around his table when the Commander walked in; he was dragging the traitor inside. He suddenly slipped off the Commander's grip and ran towards Manuel and caught hold of his feet. "Please boss, don't kill me," he said, pleading for mercy.

"It's too late, no mercy."

Manuel took the gun from the Commander's hands and started to check the number of bullets in it. The traitor slowly stood up and moved backwards. The Commander dived to catch him but he evaded him and started running. Manuel shot him without any delay. The bullet hit his back and he fell down crying in pain. Manuel walked to him. The traitor was crying out in pain. Manuel gave a soft kick. The traitor stammered and said, "I am sorry."

"Too late," Manuel said and pumped rest of the five bullets into his stomach. Blood flowed in the ground. The Commander was surprised to see his boss in such anger. He went to him and asked, "Boss, is everything all right?"

"No, where is Fisher? Where is he?"

Suddenly a man entered the room. He was taken aback to see a man killed and all the blood splattered around "Commander, call somebody to clean up this mess," he looked at the man who had entered, "and what do you want?," he asked.

"Boss, I…….I…." he stammered, looking at his angry face.

"Go on spit it out."

"I have a bad news," he said quickly and started moving back.

"And how bad is it?"

"Fisher is dead. Jimmy killed him."

"What! This is not possible."

"But boss, this is true. He killed him in your house at Paris and took away the file which you had asked."

A few men walked in. They were carrying mops and buckets of water and behind them was the Commander. He was ordering them to finish the work quickly clear out.

"Are you okay boss," Commander asked trying to talk to him but he did not respond. There was a moment of silence. Then Manuel gave the Commander the empty gun and said ""Fisher is killed but now I want you to kill Jimmy. Shoot him with whatever way you want. Do it and finish him. I want him dead by tomorrow."

"Yes boss," he said boldly.

"And why are you standing there?" he asked the man.

"Boss I have something to tell you."

"And what is it?"

"Your drugs partner, Naresh."

"Yes, what about him?"

"He is meeting the police DGP."

"So?"

"He is going to reveal our business funds and secrets to him. He said I have sold enough of drugs."

"Do you have a gun?" he asked.

"Yes sir, I have it."

"Kill him, kill Naresh, I want him dead and if you do that you will get your reward."

"Ok boss, I will do as you say."

After the conversation the man left. The cleaning staff finished doing their job. Manuel turned and picked up a bag and gave it to them.

"Take this; it has a few gold bars, share it amongst yourself."

"Thank you Boss."

Saying so, the cleaning staff members went out, feeling happy and they were fighting over the bag.

"Commander," Manuel shouted.

"Yes boss," he came running towards him.

"Book my tickets for Chennai. I am going there right away."

Chapter 12

AFTER A LONG WAIT at a junction the car moved slowly. Trying to pick up some speed and then it slowly moved leftwards. A small narrow avenue was sighted by the driver. Jimmy saw numerous boards at the starting of the road.

The driver slowly turned the car into the avenue. Going at a low speed, jimmy was getting nervous. With his heart racing, there were apartments only on one side. After driving a few metres the car stopped. Jimmy collected his things from the car and got out. The driver stepped on the pedal and rode away straight ahead and turned right. Jimmy stood silent gazing at his school. The Pilsburg High School stood four stories high. It was in the shape of a straight U. He was feeling very happy to see his old school. Beside the school was the Pilsburg auditorium and behind was the Pilsburg Arts and Science College.

Jimmy was observing the probable changes but he couldn't notice any. He felt a cold hand touching his shoulders. He turned about and saw a brown man standing behind him. His hair was shabby. His beard was growing and kept a small moustache. His nose was long and a small red spot at the end. Jimmy was trying to recognise him, while they had a warm handshake.

"You must be Ankit if I am not mistaken," he said seeing his old sonata watch. "So you finally recognised me," he replied. They looked at each other and gave a big hug.

"What are you doing here, man?" Ankit asked.

"Nothing dude, just working on a case. I think it is related to the Pit."

"Oh, I see, so you are going to see the pit right away."

"I am but if you care to join me, it would be great."

"Sure, why not, when I want to see that dreadful area."

Both of them walked forward, opening the gate of the auditorium. There was sand at the entrance and they walked past it. There were stone tiles for a few distances and then a muddy region. Jimmy walked slowly looking around; Motorbikes and scooters were parked beside him. There was a beautiful lawn on other side. Jimmy kept walking and he stepped on the muddy region. It had lots of puddles and potholes. He kept avoiding it.

"See, where you were in the last eight months." Ankit asked putting his hands in his pocket.

"Well, I was in Colombo finding a terrorist, but he escaped and then a report came that he was arrested by the Lankan Police."

"How's your sister Jim?"

"She is doing well. She is at our uncle's."

The conversation continued. They reached the rear side of the auditorium. The ground was swamp and a weird smell swayed in the air. In front of him was a garbage bin which was made of bricks and concrete. At the right corner of the bin, stood a big tree. It was full of garbage and some of it was scattered on the ground. There was a compound wall behind the bin.

"Same as it was eight years ago, nothing has changed."

"Yup nothing has changed, except for that," Ankit said pointing at the pit.

Adjusting his shirt, Ankit ran towards the wall. He kept one leg on the bin and jumped up over the wall with a split of a second. "It's your turn Jim," Ankit said.

Jimmy stood there for a while, looking at the bin. He moved forward and climbed the side wall of the bin. He saw ants creeping on the compound wall. He placed his hands on the wall and slowly climbed over it and jumped over to the other side.

"So, finally, you made it."

"Yup, I did."

They were standing in the forest region of the college. There were trees and plants all over the place. A small way, lead to the rear gate of the auditorium but it was locked. Jimmy turned right and saw Ankit looking at the saplings. He moved forward near the gate and stopped.

There was a huge tree creeping from the ground and below it was the 'pit'. Jimmy moved again and jumped into the pit. It was not very deep. Its height was the same as the length of his legs. He kept looking down. Suddenly Ankit also jumped into the pit.

"Careful buddy, I am standing here," Jimmy said balancing himself.

"Sorry, if you are looking for the door it's right below your legs."

"Thank You," Jimmy replied and moved away. Ankit bent down and cleared the leaves and dirt. A small steel door was spotted by Jimmy. Ankit kneeled down. Opening the hatch, he pulled the door with all his energy and lifted it. He dropped the door on the other side and got up.

Jimmy gave a blind clap and moved in. His eyes grew big as he saw down the tunnel. It was dark and deep.

"Who's going in first?" asked Ankit.

"Well that will be me."

"As you wish. I will take care from outside."

Jimmy dusted his pants and kneeled down searching for a ladder but didn't find it. He looked at all possible corners but he failed.

"Dude, where is the ladder?" Jimmy asked looking at Ankit drops of sweat were dropping down the ground. Ankit put his hands inside his pocket and pulled out a torch.

"Here take this rope. I am going to get something. Ankit lifted himself and ran back towards the wall, climbed it again and disappeared.

Jimmy looked at the opening. He switched on the torch and started to look for the rope. He noticed a cylindrical tunnel which led down. Patches of algae bloomed on it. He flashed the light searching for the rope but he couldn't spot it.

'Where is the rope?' he asked himself. Observing the tunnel, he kept looking at it and suddenly spotted something moving in the tunnel. "There it is," he kept the torch inside his pocket and he lay on the ground and moved his hands in the tunnel and tried to reach out for the rope.

♪   ♪   ♪

Fifteen minutes later, Jimmy was inside the tunnel making his way to the bottom of it moving slowly and steadily. He crawled down the wall using the rope. Sweat was dripping down from his forehead. He then left the rope and jumped once he neared the bottom.

He was on his feet, as soon as he had jumped. Rubbing the sweat from his head, he tied his shoe lace and moved forward. He stopped for a moment, trying to see the corridor. He looked into his pocket and took out the torch and flashed it.

Jimmy spotted a black door in front of him. He flashed the torch up and down, trying to remember the past happenings. The whole corridor had tiny holes by which air could come in but he knew he had to finish his work quickly and go back to Mumbai,

Jimmy stood there looking at the door. He moved forward and kept his hands on the door knob, turned it and entered the room.

Chapter 13

C ATHERINE GOT OUT OF the cab and handed the driver a hundred rupee note and he drove away. Catherine was worried her cousin was not picking up her call and she rolled her eyeballs and turned about.

'Neela apartment' was the name of the nine storied building. Catherine stood beside the gate gazing at the tall structure. She had noticed such vague colour patterns on the building which was not so common in Mumbai.

She moved in, keeping her phone inside but, she constantly kept thinking about Jimmy.

"Excuse me Ma'am, whom do you want to meet?" asked the security guard. He held a club on his hand which he used to play with. He wore a blue security uniform and had a star on his dress.

"I have come to see Mr. Naresh."

"Just a minute ma'am. I will call him on the intercom and let you know."

The guard was having a long conversation and Catherine kept on waiting. She looked around the building premises.

At a distant corner, she could see garbage thrown out and spread out on the ground. There were flies and dogs that were scampering for food.

The guard kept down the phone and turned towards Catherine. "Ma'am, you can go and meet him. Flat no. 21, 2nd floor, 1st block."

"Thank you," said Catherine and moved into the lift which went up noiselessly.

She pushed the lift door open and walked out of the lift. In front of her was a small board on the all which read "2nd floor." She looked left and right on the corridor, looking for the apartment.

"Catherine," shouted a man from a flat on the left wing. A five footed man stood beside the door of the house. He waved his hands at her and went back inside the house leaving the door open.

Catherine looked stunned. She stood silent for a while and then she walked through the hallway and stopped in front of the house. She quickly opened the strap of her sandals and entered the house bare footed.

The house was dirty and shabby. Clothes were scattered around the house. Beer bottles lay on the floor. Naresh stood beside his dining table pouring a drink in his glass. He added a few ice cubes and sat on a chair.

"Ah! Catherine," he exclaimed looking at his niece he took a big gulp of his drink, leaving out the ice and kept the glass on the table.

"What do you want?," he asked her reaching out for the bottle, "will you have something hot or cold?."

"Uncle, I just want to know what you are going to tell the Commissioner."

"So, you want to know about my business."

"Yes uncle please help me."

"Ok, look," he said pointing out at his TV. Behind the TV there is a file."

Catherine turned around and looked at the TV. Moving swiftly, she jumped over the sofa and landed just a foot away from the TV.

"Good stunt," Naresh said. He opened up the bottle again and started to pour it in the glass and drank it all in a gulp again.

The area around the TV was cramped, Catherine tried to reach out for the file but she failed. She kept extending her hands to grab it. Then she brought her hands back, gave a look at her uncle who was happily drinking. She waited for a while to catch her breath and then she lifted up the big TV but she was not able to pull it out. So she started to move the things on the floor to one side and slowly she moved forward grabbed the file from the rear end of the TV.

She felt tired and exhausted. Leaving the TV on the floor, she went back to the dining table and kept the file on it. "Here's the file, now what?" Catherine demanded. Naresh put his glass down, handed over the file to Catherine and said, "Read the file, you will get the answers for all your queries."

*   *   *

Jimmy kept walking down the stairs. But he was alert. Since his descend down the stairs, he had been hearing footsteps. But when he turned around to check who it was, but he didn't find anyone however he continued to hear the footsteps.

"I think my ears are ringing," he said and continued to walk. The sound of the footsteps grew louder and fast approaching him. Jimmy stopped. He waited for the noise to stop. Sensing a person behind him, he removed his gun from the holster and immediately turned back.

"Aye Jimmy! Cool down," Ankit said, covering his face. Jimmy was slashing light on Ankit's face. "Jim, put down the torch." Jimmy turned the torch downwards and Ankit was normal again.

"Where were you? Jimmy asked,
"Sorry boss, but I just went to get you some information."
"And what is it?"

After the construction of the underground rail Clarke's men had been digging from subway station."

"So, you are saying they were digging a tunnel?"

"Yup, and I believe, they were connecting the tunnel to the caves."

"Ok, so we have to be alert."

"Yes, so that's why, I brought this box."

Ankit handed over the box to Jimmy, who was looking perplexed. Jimmy handed over the torch to him and opened the box.

"What is this thing? Jimmy asked, looking at the box there was a small pipe and a narrow entry at an end. Small metal balls occupied space at a corner and a soft cloth below it for covering.

"This Jim is an old fashioned gun. Its bullet velocity is kind of slow but it kills a man in a single shot."

"Hmm, nice gun, well let's continue our descent without wasting any more time."

"You are right, let's move."

They kept walking down for minutes and Jimmy was tired but Ankit had his eyes searching for the door. He saw Jimmy strolling down the stairs but he did not find any.

"Jim, look there, it is a door," Ankit said with a smile on his face.

"Yes, I can see it."

"Then, what are we waiting for, let's go."

Jimmy and Ankit ran down the last stretch of stairs. They were slightly out of breath after walking down all the stairs. Jimmy gave a quick glance over his watch which ticked half past three.

Ankit entered first followed by Jimmy. But Jimmy stood astonished. Everything which he had seen eight years ago were in the respective order. Jimmy moved left and saw a big generator. He held a lever of generator and pulled it down with a great force.

It made a terrible noise but after it had stopped, the motor had started and in a quick second all the lights turned on. He looked at the generator. On top of it read 'Airo'. He turned front and looked around the room.

The room was a big cave. Lights and bulbs hung from the top. In some place there were only wires. Just beside him, there was a rail road over which a small carriage was placed but it was empty. Beside the carriage there was a big green cloth which covered a big pile of stuff.

"Jim what is that?" Ankit asked pointing at the pile.

"I don't remember," Jimmy replied quickly.

Ankit moved forward and put his hands on the cloth. He felt a smooth surface. Jimmy also moved towards it. While Ankit was still looking at it, Jimmy stood just beside him. Ankit pulled the cloth swiftly and put it down. Dust particles left the cloth and were suspended in air. Jimmy had coughed for a while and then opened his eyes.

Jimmy could not believe the scene which he was seeing. He stood stunned and saw Ankit doing the same; He saw his right side and spotted even more of these piles.

Chapter 14

"**G**OLD!" EXCLAIMED ANKIT. HE couldn't believe his eyes. He ran sideways and kept removing the cloth from all the piles. Finally he walked and stood beside Jimmy and started counting the number of piles of gold.

"Jim, a total of ten piles of gold bar whose individual weight is 10 kgs and there are approximately 500 in each. Whoever will have it, he will be a millionaire.

"I know, but this isn't for what we have come here. I am looking for clues that can tell me where Manuel is hiding."

"So, where do you think it will be," Ankit asked giving a clap.

"Well, eight years ago, there was a cupboard in which Clarke kept his valuables but I don't see it now."

"Where did you see the cupboard exactly?"

"If I had known I wouldn't have told you to search for it."

"Ok, then tell me where would you go looking for the file first?" Ankit said and then a long silence in the mine. Jimmy looked around searching for a place where he could find the file.

"Look there Ankit," Jimmy said pointing his fingers towards a wall of the cave.

"What's so special about the wall, Jim?"

"There's a door there."

"But I don't see any door?"

Jimmy ran towards the wall and started tapping it. Ankit looked on. He thought Jimmy had lost his mind.

"Ankit," Jimmy shouted at the top of his voice.

"Look here, I found the door."

Jimmy put pressure on his thumb and pressed the wall. The wall opened. Ankit stood surprised. He couldn't believe that behind the wall, a secret room was present.

"But, Jimmy, how did?"

"Well, eight years ago, when I came here to collect evidence on Clarke, somebody had hit me and I fainted. When I woke up, I saw Clarke closing the wall."

"Good thought, I will see what is inside the cupboard."

Ankit moved in and entered the room. There were photos and tools inside the room. Beside the tools was the cupboard. Painted maroon in colour, the cupboard wasn't that tall. Ankit moved further, keyed in the password and got his grip on the handle of the door.

"Wait," said Jimmy, putting his hands inside his pocket. "How did you know the password for the cupboard"?

"What do you mean"?

"Since Clarke's escape, his men have entered the cave and used it for mining. They would have changed the password of the cupboard as they knew that we were there."

"I just made a guess."

"Ankit, the truth please."

"Which truth… I….don't…" he stammered and continued to do. Meanwhile he tried to open the cupboard.

"Ankit clam down and tell the truth," he stood there silent and then removed his hands and turned towards Jimmy who looked at him sternly.

"Two days ago, Manuel's aide paid a visit to my house. He told that you might be coming to visit the caves. He told me to grab a file which was inside this cupboard and give it to him and threatened me.

"Then why didn't you take it?"

"I didn't know where the file was?"

"Ok fine, give me the file, let's go to Mumbai together, you'll be safe.

"Not so fast," called a voice from behind.

Jimmy and Ankit quickly turned to search for the source of the sound. They saw they were surrounded with men with a gun in their hands. They could hear footsteps and then in front of them appeared a black man with a red hair over his head. He wore black shirt and a brown pant. His sun shades were seen hanging out from his pocket. His hands had lot of colourful rings.

"Hello boys, welcome to the mine, we meet again."

"Hello, Mr. Clarke. I believe you recognise me?"

"How can I forget the small boy who was about to put me behind bars and you Ankit, can't you do such a small thing. I just asked for a file.

"Why did I give the duty to you," slapping his head, "you haven't changed all these years."

"Why have you come back?" asked Jimmy.

"Look who's asking. You know why I am here, now hand it over Jimmy."

Not so easily, tell me 'uncle' why did you kill Manuel?"

"I told you so many times. Years ago, aye, and don't call me uncle and killing of Manuel is a long story."

"Make it short and take your file."

"People, what you doing are waiting for, grab that file."

There were 20 men who advanced Jimmy and Ankit. They all had guns in their hands. Clarke was waiting for his men to get the file as he had to return. His men were closing in at Jimmy and Ankit. Jimmy was moving back and then stopped. He was moving back and then stopped. He was leaning on the wall. The armed men kept moving forward.

"Stop!" Jimmy said.

"What's the matter Jimmy, are you scared?"

Jimmy put his hands inside his pockets and picked out a small case which was in the shape of a cutting glass cover.

"Ah! Jim, you want to die with your glasses. Men, grab the file."

Jimmy quickly switched a red button which was present on the case. The case suddenly expanded and it started growing fat and after a few seconds, it was as big as a machine gun with rods protruding and a long belt of bullets was attached to its tail.

"Put down your guns, people," Jimmy said placing his hands over the trigger. "And hand over the guns," Ankit said who was trying to boost his confidence. Slowly and steadily everyone put their guns down and pushed it towards Ankit. He picked them up and loaded them in the cupboard and locked it.

"Ok, now everyone will move inside this secret compartment silently," Jimmy said moving towards the rail track. All the men moved in except for Clarke. He was searching his gun inside his coat.

"Okay uncle, at the count of three, you will come to us otherwise I will shoot you."

"You know, whenever I want my gun, I don't find it," Clarke said raising his elbows bent. He walked in a peculiar way as if something was hitting him in the knees.

"What are you doing? Can't you walk properly? "Ankit asked.

"I think something stuck in my pants," Manuel said as he continued to struggle with his pants.

"Hey Jim," Ankit whispered in Jimmy's ear, "Let's walk away from here before he does something. Remember this happened at that that time too."

"Yeah, you're right, let's run."

Secretly, Jimmy and Ankit moved to the other side from where they entered, while Clarke was still fighting with his pants. Clarke had his hands inside his pants, trying to get to his knees. Jimmy and Ankit turned back and ran towards the exit.

Clarke looked up and then there was loud "thud" on the ground. He and all his men looked down at it and spotted a gun. "Finally," Clarke said. "I found my gun," He lifted his gun and turned towards his men.

"Why are you looking at my face, go get them, you lousy idiots." His men ran after them while he was still looking around the place.

⚜   ⚜   ⚜

Jimmy and Ankit were seated in a car and Ankit was telling the driver to leave them at the airport.

"That was close, wasn't it?" Jimmy said.

"Yup, that was."

Jimmy took out his phone and switched it on. His face was sweating.

"Ankit, look at this, 15 missed calls from Cath."

"Hmm, she is really missing you."

Chapter 15

CATHERINE WATCHED JIMMY AND Ankit walking towards the exit of Chatrapati Shivaji airport. Both Ankit and Jimmy had a single backpack on their shoulders. Catherine waited for Jimmy to come out as she wanted to pounce on him and beat him up for not picking her calls.

"Hi Catherine, how long have you been waiting?" Jimmy said as he made a swift exit and was ready to leave for the parking area.

"Where were you for the last 16 hours, I had been trying to call you."

"Well, I am sorry for that. Ankit and I had a little mix up with Clarke."

"Hi Catherine, long time," Ankit said extending his hands for a shake.

"Hi! Ankit. Really long time," she responded shaking hands with him.

"So, let's move, the car is standing, let's go." After having seated comfortably in the car, Catherine took over the wheels and started the engine. Jimmy and Ankit placed their backpacks on their lap and Catherine stepped on the accelerator.

"So Jim, did you get something useful?"

"Kind of, we got a file on the financial business of Manuel, but still no clue about his hiding place."

"But Jim, we met Clarke, so we could have asked him," Ankit said who was trying to get his place in the conversation.

"Ankit, you met Clarke, it means that Manuel is dead."

"Catherine, you are wrong, we didn't meet Clarke," Jimmy said as he was thinking.

"But Jim, he was Clarke when we met back here."

"No. He wasn't Clarke, Ankit. I say so because as far as I know Clarke, he never wore rings and did you see that person. He had his fingers covered with rings."

"Then why were you talking to him as if he was Clarke?" Ankit asked as his curiosity grew big.

"At the first moment, I thought it was Clarke but just as we were making our exit, I saw his rings. The man we saw back there was probably wearing a mask and was sent by Manuel to kill but he ended up acting like Clarke."

"So, what now, where will we find Manuel's hiding place?," asked Catherine who was not interested in driving but to hear Jimmy.

"Ah!, I don't know," responded Jimmy. "But I know a person who might know."

"Who is it?" Ankit asked.

"You will get to know about the place tomorrow morning, for now stop the car. I will meet you tomorrow at Shivaji Park at 8.00 a.m. sharp. Please don't call unless it is very urgent."

Saying so, Catherine stopped the car letting Jimmy get off the car. He bid adieu and walked away the opposite direction while Catherine and Ankit drove away to the safe house.

❧   ❧   ❧

Manuel was sitting on his chair waiting for the arrival of his Commander. The rest of his men were loading a truck full of drugs which was supposed to be transported all over the city.

"Boss, the truck is loaded," said a man who came running to him.

"That's good, now take the truck and deliver it where I have asked you to go."

The man agreed and made fast exit from the room when another man entered.

"Boss, the shipment has arrived. It has 20 boxes full of drugs," he said.

"Very good. Bring it to the base," replied Manuel.

When the conversation was going on, another man entered the room with a big smile on his face.

"Boss, 50 boxes of gold has arrived to our base from Chennai."

"Excellent job. Now start the work that has been assigned to you and any news about the Commander?'

"Yes sir, he is outside."

"Then bring him in, I need to have a word with him."

Minutes passed and the Commander entered the room slowly. He looked tired, his hair was in disarray, he wore a black shirt but it was wrinkled. His pants were covered with mud. His head looking down signalling Marvel that he has failed. He moved in and put his hands back.

"So, Commander, how did you finish the mission?"

"No sir, neither could I get the file nor could I kill the agents."

"What happened at the mine"?

"I went dressed like Clarke and ended acting like Clarke."

"No problem, as far as you get the gold, you will be rewarded only for that."

"Thanks boss," he said managing a smile on his face.

Manuel pulled the drawer of his desk and took out his gun. While he was loading the bullets, the Commander was punishing himself for the failure. When he gave a glance at Manuel he pulled the trigger and shot 4 bullets at his chest. The Commander immediately fell down dead instantly. Blood flowed on the floor.

"Call the cleaning staff," he shouted looking at the dead body which lay on the floor.

★   ★   ★

Senior Inspector Rout sped inside the police station. The police station was painted yellow. He was in the same uniform which he was wearing for the last 3 days. He had forgotten about day and night since his first major case after his promotion.

Today, he was very happy as he had caught the criminal. His team was pleased with his efforts and thinking abilities which helped them to nab the person. He was on his way back after his friends threw a party for him. He was in a hurry, he ran across the corridors as the Commissioner was waiting for him in his cabin.

Just as he was going to enter his cabin, he tipped over the shoe lace and fell down. There was a loud noise. He got up slowly and entered his cabin dusting his shirt and hands. Immediately, after he looked at the Commissioner, he lifted his hands and gave a bold salute.

The Commissioner was well in his fifties. His hair had shades of grey and his skin started to have a few wrinkles. The uniform which he wore was clean and crisp. He held his cap in his hands and was looking at Rout with his brown eyes.

"Sir, you summoned me," said Rout with a polite tone. He looked nervous and was anxious.

"Yes, Rout, I wanted to congratulate you for nabbing the criminal.

Suddenly a big smile emerged from Rout's mouth. He was happy as his nervousness was gone.

"Now Rout, don't be really very happy. I want you to come to Naresh's house. He has to give his statement and also bring the typist.

Rout agreed to it and gave a big smile. When he was about to leave the Commissioner stopped him again. "Rout, first you go home and have a bath, you're stinking right now. We will meet here exactly after an hour.

Rout gave another smart salute and walked away towards his jeep. He was happy to see the Commissioner appreciate him for his job. He thought that he had taken a very good decision of joining the police force. He started to remember his academy where he trained to become what he was a successful police officer.

❧ ❧ ❧

Catherine stopped the car. She had been driving since an hour. Due to the heavy traffic, she had to stop at a junction for about twenty minutes. Ankit opened the door, but he was in no mood to walk as his legs were hurting him. He could barely walk. Catherine was worried about Jimmy. He gave strict instruction not to talk to him till he got some clues about the hiding place of Manuel.

"So Ankit, what's your plan for the evening."

"I am going to get some good sleep."

"What about you," asked Ankit.

"Reassess the clues and paper. I think I might find something."

"All the best," Ankit said entering the house. He quickly removed his shoes and went straight into a room and locked it.

Catherine sat on the sofa and switched on the TV relaxing her mind. As there was nothing interesting, she switched it off and dozed away sitting on the sofa.

Chapter 16

A POLICE CAR STOPPED IN front of Neela apartments. Inspector Rout came out and opened the back door. The Police SP came out of the car. He was in his late 50's and had only 3 months left for his retirement. His hair had a salt and pepper look, wore his favourite shining black shoes and was in his uniform. As soon as he walked away from the car, Rout closed the door and all the cars left the place, except one.

The guard of the building saluted the officer and asked them, "What can I do for you."

"We have come to meet Naresh," Rout said and the guard quickly gave them the direction to his house. Rout thanked him and he walked slowly along with the DGP and his bodyguards.

"Can I have a word with Rout," the SP asked.

"Yes sir," he replied.

"Rout, how did you solve the murder case in three days?"

"Well Sir, it was just the matter of hard work and dedication, but now the case will go on and on in the Court."

"I agree with that, Rout," he said as they approached the elevator.

The elevator was already at the ground floor and they entered it. Rout pressed the button of second floor softly and the elevator started to climb.

"Sir, how many cases have you solved so far," Rout asked with a curious look on his face.

"Not many, just about 100 and in most cases the culprit gets either a bail or he is judged guilty by the Court."

The elevator stopped with soft bump. Rout opened the doors and the men trouped out. They turned left and walked straight down the corridor. They went past house no. 15 and kept moving. They all spotted house no. 21 at the same time. But Rout was cautious. He noticed the door was open.

"Guards, Be alert," Rout whispered as he removed his gun.

Rout was feeling tensed up as he moved towards the house, his gun in his hands. Rout leaned towards the wall beside the house. He waved his hand which gave a signal to the guards telling them to come towards the house.

Just as they moved towards the house, Rout quickly tip toed into the house. The house was dark. He was searching the switch board when DGP entered with his guard. He was calling out Naresh's name and Rout found the switches. Suddenly the SP called out Rout and said, "Rout I see someone there." Listening to him, Rout switched the first button from right which lighted the tube light.

Everything was seen clear. Rout turned back. He couldn't utter even a single letter from his mouth. He saw a man standing behind the sofa. He wore a blue shirt, his hair was shabby, his shirt had wrinkles and he was sweating a lot.

"Who are you?" asked Rout as he saw the man.

"I ...." he stammered.

"What's that in your hand?" Rout asked again but didn't reply. Rout walked towards him. The DGP was still standing beside the main door with the guards and was watching Rout going towards the man. As he approached him, he moved backwards but didn't have any place to go.

Rout stopped beside him. The man was wearing black pants and he was holding a knife which was covered with blood and it was dripping on the floor.

"Great Gods," Rout said as he bent down. He saw a body, stabbed twice in the stomach. Rout was shocked. He lifted the man's hands and checked his pulse. But he was dead. He stood up and saw the DGP shook his head and said,

"Sir, Naresh is dead."

"What? Are you sure," the SP said and he moved swiftly towards the body and saw it lay on the ground and the blood oozing from the wound. Rout took out a plastic cover from his pocket and opened it. At the centre of the cover in yellow it was written "evidence" and told the man in blue shirt to put the knife into it. He told the guards to call the ambulance quickly and handed over the knife to one of the guards.

Rout took out a pair of handcuffs and put it on the man's hands.

"What are you doing?" asked the man.

"Arresting you for the murder of Naresh."

"You can't do that, I am innocent."

"Don't tell that to me buddy, prove it in the Court. I am just doing my job," Rout said as he moved the man outside the house.

"My lawyer will prove that I am innocent," the man said with an angry face.

"All the best," Rout said as he took him inside the elevator and he pressed the button for the ground floor. The elevator moved down quickly. The man was looking angry.

Back at the police station, Rout was pulling the man inside and forcibly made him sit on a chair beside his desk. He rubbed his hands over his forehead. The man constantly kept telling Rout that he was innocent.

As soon as he sat down on his chair, a constable brought him a glass of water and also offered some to the man but he refused. Rout called out for another constable who pulled out a chair and attached a paper to the typewriter.

"So now tell me what is your name?, asked Rout.

"It's Jimmy."

"Full name."

"I don't have any."

"Your occupation"

"Just a sales agent for soaps."

"Describe the things you saw at Naresh's house as you say you are innocent."

"Today evening, Uncle Naresh called me up and asked me to meet him. The security guard saw me and told me to go inside as he was already instructed. When I reached his house, I saw the door open and so entered inside. The house was dark with no light. When I looked around, I saw a man's shadow. He was probably holding a file. I went towards to him but I tripped and fell down."

Rout was closely listening to him and the typist was typing fast in the computer noting down his statement. "When I got up I saw Naresh's body lying on the ground. The man came close holding a knife and suddenly he threw the knife at me. I caught it. I stared at my uncle's face as he lay dead. Then the lights were switched on and that's when I saw you guys."

"That's a nice story over there."

"It's isn't a story. It is the truth."

"Umm, okay, if it is the truth, then you need to wait for a while. If my men get evidence which is against your story then I will lock you up," Rout said as he ordered the typist to leave the room and told him over his statement. He was going through the statement when a sub inspector entered his room and said "Sir, we have got evidence."

"What is it?"

"Sir, we have got a hankie, this pen and a shirt button. I have the fingerprint report of the knife, the button and the pen."

"What does it say?"

"Sorry Sir, I haven't opened it yet."

"No problem, leave it on the table, I will check it. So Jimmy, let me see your shirt, is this your shirt's button?"

"I don't think so," Jimmy replied. But Rout wasn't satisfied. He checked his shirt and found a button missing. He opened the evidence cover and took out the button using gloves and tried to match it.

"Perfect match," he said, "Is this pen yours?"

"Yes, it is mine, but I did not have it in my pocket today."

"And what about the hankie?"

"That's also mine but I had kept this in my house under my bed. I don't know how it got there."

"Well after seeing the evidence it is all against you. I am afraid I have to lock you up."

"I need to speak to my lawyer."

Chapter 17

C ATHERINE WOKE UP WITH a start. She was desperate to know about the findings of Jimmy. After four hour sleep on the couch she was feeling relaxed but her feet were paining. Suddenly there was a loud noise. When she looked around, she realised that it was the Cuckoo clock. She saw the time and it read '10:30' in the night.

She reached out for her phone and switched it on. There was a surprise look on her face as she saw five missed calls of Jimmy. Without further thought she rang him up. The phone kept ringing for a long time and then the call was received.

"Hello Jim, what happened? Why did you call me," Catherine said as she hesitated on the line. She looked tense as there was no answer from the other side.

"Hello, this is inspector Rout. Who is speaking?"

"This is Catherine, Jimmy's sister. Where is he?"

"Miss, Jimmy has been locked up. He is accused of murder."

"What? ....What are you saying."

"Meet me at my office in Dadar."

"I am coming right away."

⚜ ⚜ ⚜

Manuel was staring at his men as they were working continuously from morning. They had been loading and unloading crates which had packets of drugs. He was trying to manage a smile as his men were helping him establish an empire in India. He was remembering his days when he was working hard in France selling drugs.

A tall man walked towards Manuel. His hair neat and well oiled. He was holding a red file in his hands. His face was glowing due to the rays of the sun. He had blue eyes and a long pointed nose. He stopped in front of Manuel and handed over the file to him

"Boss, Jimmy has been arrested for the murder of Naresh. He has been locked up. All the evidences are against him. There's no one who can stop us now"

"That's great news Eric. Behind the chair I have kept your reward. Take it"

"Thanks boss, but I didn't get it?"

"Didn't get what?"

"Jimmy had travelled around the world in search of 4 files. What is important in those files?"

"A few years ago when Clarke and I were working together he had stolen few files from the secret agency. When he came to Paris to meet me he stole documents regarding my business and hid them.

"So I don't understand?"

"He stole them when I wanted to start my trade in India. So in one of those files I had written the address of my contacts and my other secrets. If they get hold of that file then I might go to jail."

"Don't worry boss. I will make sure that they don't get the file."

ॐ   ॐ   ॐ

Catherine made a swift entrance into the police station. She calmed herself and she went towards an inspector. "I have come to meet jimmy, Inspector"

"Ah! You must be Catherine. Please have a seat" Rout said as he saw her. He put away a file and made himself comfortable"

"Inspector, he could not have committed this crime"

"But miss, we have evidence against him"

"He is just holding a high post in the government office"

"Yes. He told me that he is a sales agent"

"We just came here for holidays and he went to meet uncle to get some important contacts for our business."

"Even if I trust you, I can't release him; I have evidences that point towards Jimmy. He is to be shown before the magistrate tomorrow."

"Fine, I will call a lawyer, but can I at least meet him?"

"Sorry but the meeting timings are over. You can come tomorrow"

"Thank you" was the last word uttered by Catherine to the inspector and left the place with a saddened face.

Catherine took out her mobile and dialled a foreign number. She looked desperate as she waited for the receiver to pick up the call and the she heard a person speak. "Hello ---- remember me ---- need your help ---- can you fly to India ---- my brother's in trouble" she said and disconnected the line.

Catherine sat inside her car and drove away. She drove slow and steady moving across traffic signals, worrying about Jimmy. An hour later, she reached her house. She felt tired and just wanted to doze off to sleep.

❧ ❧ ❧

Catherine was standing beside the walls of the arrival gate of the Mumbai airport. She was observing the maids as they were sweeping the floor. Many people standing there covered their faces to protect themselves from the dust.

Suddenly the arrival gate opened and at a distance she saw a man holding a brown suitcase.

She walked forward and waved her hand. The man gave her a quick reply by waving back and came to her quickly.

"Hello Fisher, how are you........."

❧   ❧   ❧

Jimmy entered the court room along with 3 constables. He was handcuffed while he was being brought inside. The constables stopped him and unlocked the cuffs and told him to stand in the accused box. He walked forward but his face was looking down.

And suddenly there was a call announcing the arrival of the judge and he entered the room. He kept pushing his specs on his nose and he sat on his chair. Jimmy could see the bald pate but yet he was in no mood for a laugh. He saw the lawyers table and saddened even more as there was no lawyer appointed to him.

"Where's the defense lawyer?" asked the judge to jimmy but there was no answer from his side. When the judge was about to ask again, a tall man entered the room. He was adjusting his coat and kept a file on the table. He went forward to the judge and immediately apologised for his delay and handed over some documents needed for the case and took his seat. The Judge went through the documents.

"Let the proceedings begin" said the judge and the prosecutor stood up and cleared his throat

"My lord, 2 days ago this person who is standing in the accused box went to meet his uncle. He lived alone and his name was Naresh. Naresh was getting ready as the SP had an appointment with him. Naresh was a drug dealer. Jimmy went inside silently and stabbed him on his back." he said boldly. He went back to the table and pulled out a paper from a file and handed it to the typist who handed it to the judge.

"My Lord, the paper you are holding is the post mortem report which says that Naresh was stabbed by the knife which is kept on the evidence table." He pulled out another paper and showed it to the Judge and said, "This is the fingerprint report which reads that the fingerprint on the knife has an exact match of Jimmy's. All evidences are against this man, that's all, my Lord."

The public prosecutor turned and went back towards his seat. The Defense lawyer got up. He took a pen from his pocket and started to walk towards the public prosecutor. He drew a line in his hand and threw the pen towards his counterpart who caught it with a single hand.

"I object my Lord; defense lawyer is playing games in the Court."

"It's no game; you can see that the public prosecutor drew on my hand. Look, he is holding the pen in his hand."

"What do you mean by that, you drew it? What do you want to prove?"

"I just want to say that there was a third person inside the house who threw the knife at my client like the way I did to the prosecutor, that's all, my Lord."

The Prosecutor stood up and said "Your Honour, now I would like to call my first witness."
"Permission granted," the Judge said.
"The watchman of the apartment."

With a smile on his face, the watchman came and stood in the witness box.

"So, you are the watchman of the apartments?" asked the prosecutor. She was holding a piece of paper in her hand.

"Yes, I am the watchman."

"Do you recognise that man who is standing over there," she said pointing to Jimmy.

"Yes, he came yesterday to meet Naresh. He was wearing the same dress and had a knife with him."

"Point to be noted, my Lord, the accused had a knife with him when he entered the victim's house, and that is the knife, that's all."

The defense lawyer stood up and approached the watchman. He looked at him with his big eyes and saw his dress which he was wearing. "Did that man over there" he said pointing at jimmy. "Had something in his hands or in his pocket?"

"Yes sir, he had a knife." The watchman said immediately without giving it a thought.

"Okay now can you tell us what type of knife was it?"

"It was a vegetable knife; he was holding it in his hand."

The defense lawyer walked the table and picked a paper from his file said

"My lord this man his lying. Here is the forensic report." He handed over the paper to the judge and continued, "The report says that the knife belonged to Naresh and he was using it for eating apples just before his death"

"So then, where was the watchman when Jimmy entered?" the prosecutor asked.

"The watchman was asleep when Jimmy entered. Because when a visitor enters the building, the watchman has to telephone the resident about him for his permission. When the police checked the call records of the intercom on that day the watchman did not call Naresh about Jimmy's entry."

Suddenly there was a ding at the wall clock which sounded the end of the hearing the judge announce the next date of the court which was 3 days later and adjourned the court. Both the lawyers bowed before the judge and shook hands and left the court.

Chapter 18

J IMMY WAS DISTRESSED. CATHERINE was seated next to him trying to comfort him. The prison door opened slowly and the lawyer entered the room. He had a notepad in his hand and a pen pinned to his shirt. He closed the door and walked to Jimmy.

"Hi Jimmy, my name is Aakash. Tell me what happened last night?"

"Whatever I saw, I have told the police."

"No, I am asking, if you saw something strange?"

"I don't think so," Jimmy replied immediately.

"Think it over and be fast."

"Jimmy thought hard. He was recollecting everything that happened last night.

"Of course," Jimmy said and he stood up with excitement. "Last night after ... he threw the knife, he sprinted across the bedroom and then outside Naresh's house, I saw two pairs of shoe lying when I entered."

"That will be enough for me, Thank you. If there is anything else do let me know."

※ ※ ※

The next day Aakash had arrived early at the Court. He was standing with Catherine who was explaining him some important happenings. When there was a pat on Catherine's shoulder. She turned about and recognised her boss.

"Mr A, what are you doing here?"

"The agency is trying it's best to release jimmy. Catherine, I want you to meet my Secretary and this young man beside her is her husband"

Catherine shook hands with both of them and she was introducing herself to the young man while Aakash went inside the courtroom.

Jimmy entered the court room along with Catherine and his boss. After everybody got settled, the Judge arrived and ordered the start of the hearing immediately after he sat down.

"My Lord," Aakash stood up and walked in front of the Judge and said, "I would like to call the Chief Inspector in charge of the case, Mr. Rout."

"Permission granted."

Rout bowed before the Judge and climbed the witness box. He took off his cap and held it in his hands, while the defence lawyer moved towards him.

"So, inspector, what happened when you turned on the light?"

"The guards, SP sir and I saw that man standing in the box, holding a knife and standing beside Naresh's body."

"Then what happened."

"I cuffed him and took him away."

"When did you search the victim's house"?

"An hour later."

"My lord, there was a third person inside the house, when the police left, that man took the opportunity of the one hour gap and ran away."

"Mr. Aakash," said the prosecutor trying to say something in the discussion. "Do you have any evidence that there was a third person?."

"My Lord, I would now like to call Mr. Verma who is the neighbour of Naresh."

"Permission granted."

The inspector walked down and paved the way for Mr. Verma. He swung his hands which hit the inspector but neither of them minded. Verma climbed on the witness box.

"Mr. Verma when you returned home after work, what did you see?"

"I saw that Naresh's house door was open and he was having drinks with a friend. An hour later, I saw two pairs of shoe beside the door. One belonged to Naresh and the other probably belonged to his friend."

"My Lord, this proves my theory that there was a third person in that house."

"But that does not prove that your client is innocent" the prosecutor said. My Lord, all the evidences are against him. He had a motive of murder then why are we not treating it as an open and shut case."

"My Lord, the public prosecutor has not produced any eye witness saying that my client is guilty and evidences can be changed and turned against my client.

"My Lord, the defence lawyer is making up stories."

Aakash moved back to his table and picked up 2 photos and handed them to the Judge.

"My Lord, these two pictures were taken in Naresh's house one before the death and one after the death. You can see a brown cupboard open in both the photos. In the photo taken before the death, you can see the clothes have been piled up inside but in the other photo you can see them neatly arranged. Please note the time at which the photo was taken. The first one was taken half an hour before the murder and the next one was taken a day later, when I was questioning the neighbour.

"What are you trying to say, Mr. Aakash?" asked the prosecutor.

"I am trying to say, when the third person killed Naresh and threw the knife to my client, he went inside the room and hid himself in the cupboard. During the gap he arranged the cupboard so that no one will suspect that somebody else was there. That's all, my Lord."

"Prosecutor, do you have anything to say."

"At this moment, no my Lord, but the prosecutor asks for time, my Lord."

"In that case the Court is willing to give time to the prosecutor and in the meantime the Court orders the police to dig deep into this case. Till then the Court is adjourned."

༄ ༄ ༄

"What happened," Manuel asked. He was seated in his chair talking to his commander who was eagerly waiting for his boss to hear the good news.

"I went to the Court today. It seemed like Jimmy will be freed but the Court was adjourned and the next date is 3 weeks from now. At this rate he will never leave the prison."

"Excellent work, Commander. Now let's talk business. What's our progress?"

"We have planned to organise parties all around the city in secret places this Sunday where every drink will have small amounts of Marijuana. This will addict them to keep taking the drug."

"Nice work Commander, take that bag over there. That is your reward. Enjoy and keep updating me."

"Yes boss, I will."

↭   ↭   ↭

"Please tell me something about Naresh like what kind of man was he," Aakash said.

"Naresh was a very kind and honest man and minded his own business," his neighbour said. "Although he never lived here most of the time, whenever he was here he used to visit his friends and neighbours spending time with them."

"Do you have any idea about his profession?"

"Yes, he said he was a sales agent."

"For the past few days, did you see or hear something unusual."

"Yes three days ago, a lady paid a visit to Naresh's house and she dropped a file. Let me see, he said as he went inside his house. Aakash looked around the house looking at the furniture and the television which was showcasing cricket matches.

"Minutes later, the man came back holding a file. He handed it over to Aakash and he left the place thanking Naresh's neighbour. Aakash kept the file into his bag and made an exit from his house looking at the interior of the house and turned his back and walked towards the staircase.

Naresh's neighbour closed the door and pulled out his mobile from his pocket and dialled a number.

"Hello Boss, it's me."

"Yes, speak up," Manuel said who was in the middle of his meal.

"Boss, Jimmy's lawyer had turned up. He was asking questions about Naresh and I gave him a fake file."

"Nice job, Commander, now relax for a few days."

〜 〜 〜

"Catherine did you visit Naresh before his death," Aakash asked as he made himself comfortable in the sofa of the safe house."

"Yes, a day before, why?"

"Did he give you a file?"

"Yes, he did, it is in my bag."

"Just, as I suspected."

"What happened?"

"Naresh's neighbour told me that he had seen a lady drop a file and then he gave a fake file. This means that the man is working for the killer."

"Then who is the killer?'

"Well, I don't know. We will have to wait for the police to gather up clues for us to work with. Till then we will have to search up Naresh's apartment."

Chapter 19

Present day……….

CATHERINE WAS SEATED ON a chair at her study. She had been writing a diary since a month. She was depressed and wouldn't talk to anyone. Her brother Jimmy was in the prison for almost three months. Jimmy had been talking less to Catherine. All their efforts to catch the drug lord had gone down the drain. No more leads, no contacts, nothing was left except for one important thing- a blue file.

"Dear Diary," Catherine wrote, it's been three months since Jimmy has gone to Jail. They have had only 5 hearings as there are no dates available for a fast and quick trial. I set out to find the blue file but all went in vain. There is a drug menace in the city and the police are unable to do anything.

A knock on the door and she put the pen down and went to open the door.

"Who is it at 2 am in the night," she thought.

She turned the knob and opened the door. It made a squeaky sound but it stopped. Aakash was standing at the entrance. He held a black book in one hand and his briefcase in other.

"What are you doing here at this time?, Catherine asked.

"Jimmy can be released. I have proof of his innocence," Aakash said with a big smile.

Catherine stood still, shocked. She recovered after a while and managed a smile.

"Are you Serious?"

"Yes, but I want to know what does this mean?' Aakash asked as he gave her a small piece of paper. Catherine took it in; she sat on the couch and stared at the paper.

"Where did you find it?"

"In Naresh's diary."

"Three months ago, Jimmy and I went in search of four files which Naresh had kept here and there. All the four are with me but none of them had any clue of the hiding place of Manuel."

"So did you find the clue?"

"Yes, you did this; it's the paper which will take us there. But who killed Naresh?"

"You will have to wait till tomorrow."

❧   ❧   ❧

"Come on boys, pack up fast, we leave tomorrow night," Manuel said clearing his desk. He stacked up his guns in a huge bag and filled up hundreds of cartons with drugs. The last shipment arrived at the same time as twenty new recruits started their work, filling up cartons.

"Boss, where are we going?" the commander asked as he entered the room.

"Leaving the place as you see, going to another city of course."

"What about Mumbai?"

"You'll take care of it. I knew that you can do the assigned works that I have given. Once you sell out 60 shipments, then you will join me in Chennai."

The commander turned and moved towards the exit but he felt a hand on his shoulder and he stopped. He saw Manuel coming to his front and standing with his hands in his pocket.

"Where are you going, help our men out in packing?"

"I am sorry boss, but I need to go to the hearing, they'll suspect me, I will return as soon as it is over."

"Fine, go home, get some rest but don't forget you have to update me."

"As you say boss" and he left the mill swiftly.

The clock struck ten in the morning and Jimmy entered the Court for the last hearing. He looked relieved and hoped that his lawyer would help him get a clean chit from the case. The prosecutor was seeing at the paper which she would use it to convict Jimmy.

Aakash entered with his briefcase and the case file in his hands and Catherine following him. He kept his briefcase on the floor and file on the table. He was about to sit but he heard the doors opening and spotted the Judge entering.

After showing respect of bowing towards the Judge, everyone sat down.

"Please start the proceedings."

"My Lord," the prosecutor said springing from her chair. She walked forward and continued. "I can see that there is no evidence that can prove that Jimmy is not the killer. Without wasting much more time of the Court, please pronounce your verdict."

"Not so fast Ms. Prosecutor," Aakash said. "Now My Lord, I will put forward certain points that will change the shape of this case. My Lord, this book."

"You are wasting the time of the Court," the prosecutor interrupted, but Aakash raised his hand to calm her down and said, "This book was found in Naresh's house and it tells us about the killer."

"What do you mean?"

"My Lord, I think you would have heard about Manuel."

"The drug Lord, why are you dragging him into this?"

"I am not dragging him, he is involved in this," Aakash said as he handed over the book to the Judge.

"My Lord, this book contains all the information about Manuel and his meetings, shipments, how many people he killed, etc. This also tells us that Naresh worked for Manuel and he was very loyal to him."

"So, this doesn't mean that Jimmy is not the killer."

"Wait for a while," Aakash said "My Lord, Naresh wanted to get out of the business, so he got settled in Mumbai. But he knew he was in trouble. So he had set up spy cameras in his house. This is the recording of the cameras," he said taking out a CD from his pocket.

"But before that, I want to say something else. The book also tells that Manuel had sent two people to bring back Naresh to the agency. But one person died two months ago in Paris. The other person is still alive and is present in the Court."

Everybody was at a shock. Mr. A, who had been listening to the debate closely was stunned. The public prosecutor had no words to say.

"My Lord, now I want to call Mr. Eric Tommenel to the witness box."

"Permission granted."

A lanky man with round spectacles stood up from the audience and walked towards the witness box. He adjusted his coat and tie and stood up on the box.

"So Mr. Eric Tommenel, how are you related to my client?"

"I am his boss's secretary's husband."

"Hmm… quite a long relation, anyway what's your occupation?"

"I work in an NGO."

"Now I will ask you a simple question and answer it straight forward. Why did you kill Naresh?"

"I object my Lord"; shouted the prosecutor, "the defense is giving false allegations about this man."

"Objection overruled."

"Thank you my Lord. Okay, now Mr. Eric, look in the book Naresh has written that Manuel will kill him and Eric might be sent to kill him. On the Judge's table there is a CD which will give us the recording of how you killed Naresh. Why are you wasting time like this"?

Eric was nervous. His sweating did not stop even after he swiped his face. He had thoughts of running away, but he knew there was Inspector Rout standing beside the witness box and all the constables guarding the exits and he had no choice left.

"Yes," shouted Eric, "I killed Naresh."

Everyone was stunned. The prosecutor, Mr. A and his secretary, Catherine and the Judge were dumbfounded. Jimmy lifted his head with surprise and had a small smile on his face. He saw Catherine who was rubbing her tears.

"Yes it is true. I killed Naresh. That fellow, he wanted to give away all the secrets of our trade to the police and the person who is smiling over there, wanted us arrested. So the simplest way was to kill Naresh and send Jimmy to Jail."

"The defense rests the case, my Lord," Aakash said boldly and stood at the centre of the Court. He stared at Jimmy who was rejoicing at the prospect of his release.

"I have questions to ask to the defense, my Lord," the prosecutor asked.

"Mr. Aakash, before the court gives its verdict I would like to see the book and the recording of the spy cam."

"I am sorry, my Lord, but the book and CD are empty. The facts about the book are correct but the spy cam is fake. I am sorry for the lies."

"Liar, you liar, you scam," Eric shouted, but he was taken away by Rout after the verdict was given.

Chapter 20

3 Days later.

"JIM, LISTEN, YOU GO left, I am going right, you have to inform Rout," Catherine said.

Jimmy and Catherine were at the back yard of the flour mill. Both of them were holding pistols and the pockets were stacked with bullets. They moved stealthy as they had decided. Jimmy moved left and then turned right at the corner, but he quickly hid himself behind cardboard boxes. He saw a few people packing boxes and placing them in the truck.

Jimmy quickly pulled out a grenade, pulled its ring and threw it with full force towards the truck. It landed at the roof of the truck. He rolled his eyes and started searching for an entry inside the mill but he didn't find any. So he went to the back yard. While on the way, he heard a boom. He stopped and peeped out and saw the truck toppled over and three men lying dead on the green cover.

Catherine saw none as she walked forward. Although she had heard a boom, she hid small smile, but did not bother. She was moving South in the West side of the mill. She stopped at the corner and peeped at the front entrance.

She saw some men, surrounding a toppled truck and boxes of drugs were scattered on the ground and there was fire around.

She turned back and traced her way back looking for an entry into the mill but she didn't find anything. She heard footsteps and a man's shadow coming from the back yard. She had her pistol ready at once but then she heard a whisper.

"Catherine, it's me, Jimmy," he whispered and came in front of her.

"No entry in the eastern side."

"Did you contact the police?" Catherine asked as she was searching for bombs in her bag.

"Yes, they said they will be here in ten minutes."

"Now let's search for an entry, come on."

Smoke filled the air. More people surrounded the truck which was ablaze. Jimmy and Catherine didn't mind the drama going on at the front. They were searching for an entry. Tapping walls, moving the leaves of the green and trying to push walls.

Meanwhile, inside the mill, Manuel was reading the morning daily when suddenly the member of his gang entered the room.

"Boss, bad news, somebody bombed the last truck of our supplies. We lost three men also."

"What? What are you saying? Didn't I tell you to seal all exits and keep a close watch on the boundaries?'

"Yes Boss. We did as you said but some of us…"

"Spit it, some of you…"

"The people who were guarding the backyard were shot."

"And why didn't you report the situation?"

"We thought they had gone to have tea."

Manuel lifted his hand and slapped the man hard. "You thought," Manuel said, "now go find Jimmy and Catherine, I am sure they are inside the compound."

The man bowed before him and ran towards the exit. Manuel was growing in anger. He crushed the newspaper in his hands and threw it on the floor. He got up kicking the chair and stood waiting for the results.

꧁ ꧁ ꧁

Jimmy pushed a grey button on the wall and from below a small passage opened. Catherine quickly pulled her gun and she went down the passage using an old ladder which was fixed to a concrete wall. Jimmy followed her but he went slowly as he didn't want to hurt his sister by going fast.

Catherine noiselessly landed on the basement. Her hand removed the torch from the belt and switched it on. Jimmy put his foot down and removed his hands from the ladder. "So, which way now?" Jimmy whispered taking out his gun again.

"Well according to the GPS, we need to move south and take the stairs."

"Seriously, where did you get Wi-Fi?"

"Welcome to the new tech age," she said proudly and walked away in search of the staircase and Jimmy followed quietly behind Catherine.

Minutes later Jimmy and Catherine were climbing up the stairs slowly and kept an eye on the top floor. "Jim, let's move quickly, the coast is clear," saying so Catherine ran over the stairs and paused at the ground floor.

Jimmy too stopped as Catherine was standing at the entrance, not allowing him to enter the room. He heard voices as he stood at the stairs. His eyes were looking at Catherine's leg, which was the only thing that he could see from his level and suddenly she disappeared from sight, a if she was pulled up.

Jimmy grew anxious as he climbed up and peeped through the door. He saw a neat floor with marble tiles, spy cameras, tables and chair arranged neatly. He could see the toppled truck and another truck arrived. A few men were waiting for it to load more cartons. He peeped to the other side and looked around. He saw a glass door opening with access control. He saw a man swipe a card and some men taking Catherine with them.

Jimmy went down to the basement and sat on a chair, trying to think of a rescue plan. He was tense and looked around. He found only garbage and broken furniture but nothing special.

❧   ❧   ❧

Catherine was walking over the marble floor. She was actually held captive by a pair of hefty men who were taking her to the main room.

"Whatever you guys are doing it's not good," Catherine said. But they ignored her. They silently held her hands and walked her forward. They had crossed two rooms which were well designed and few relics had been kept in the showcase. Catherine was surprised to see the inside design compared to the outside view of the mill.

They came across a big ancient door which looked like it had intricate design made on it. There was a biometric identifier. One of the hefty men, who seemed to be their leader, put his thumb and the door opened noiselessly.

Catherine stood and looked around to see the interior of the room. The walls were made up of black tiles and the floor was dirty with patches of blood stains as if it needed cleaning. A small wooden table was placed in the centre.

They moved in and after a few seconds the door closed again.

They made Catherine stand near the table and they walked away to different corners. She looked at them and then spotted the chair revolving and quickly moved brought her eye to see the moving chairs.

A bald headed man was seen sitting on the chair. He wore a blue shirt with a white pants and a red bow tie. His face was long with a broad chin. The table was filled with guns and ammunitions and different files.

"Ah! Catherine," he exclaimed, "I think you don't know who I am?"

"I know you, Jacques Manuel," Catherine said immediately.

"Old rivalry, new place and new techniques but alas! I think I won," Manuel said as he stood up and lifted a gun from his collection.

"It's good that you think that way because Jimmy will be here to get you."

"Do think it's easy," Manuel said. He clapped his hands and again the creaky sound was heard. Catherine turned around and saw few men carry in a young man.

"Jimmy," Catherine said as she put her hands on her head.

CHAPTER 21

Jimmy and Catherine were tied up on chairs with a brown rope. Although they struggled, they were no match to the fifty pound men. Manuel was very happy and proud of his work. But he was just waiting for the news for departure.

"So Jimmy, is there anything that I can do for you before I shoot you?" Manuel asked as he sat back on his chair while his men were cleaning the shelves and putting valuable things inside cardboard boxes.

"What happened at your house before the fire?" Jimmy asked as he struggled with the rope. Then he touched his watch and his attention went back to Manuel. "Since I sent all my servants and guards for a vacation, I went downstairs and opened the door; I was shocked to see a person standing at the porch just like me. He held a gun in his hand pointing at me. I told him to come inside and have a seat. Then he revealed that he was Clarke."

"Then why did you kill him?" Catherine interrupted.

"He was a fool. When I asked him why he was there, he shot me on my shoulder. I quickly ran outside and locked the main door. There was no way he could escape. Suddenly the whole house was up in flames. I was seeing my house ablaze from my garden. The next day, I went to Clarke's house at Nice. There I found out that he had been smuggling gold in India. So here I am."

"So you're saying that you didn't kill Clarke, then who did?" Jimmy asked curiously.

"It was a suicide. At his house he had drawn up a plan to kill me where he had written that he hired an electrician to mess up the wires.

Jimmy and Catherine looked surprised and seemed satisfied that they knew the truth. Although they still had so many questions, Manuel allowed them to ask a single question. He lifted his gun and took an aim at them. But then he stopped and said, "Wait a minute. How did you find me at the first place?"

"Long story, short version, Fisher told us," Catherine said.

"But how?" Manuel asked them as he burst out in anger.

"3 days ago," Jimmy said. "After the hearing, at the parking space of the High Court, Catherine and I were having a chat when Aakash interrupted. I looked at him and thought that I had seen him before.

"Aakash, I think I have kinda seen you."

"Of course, we met in Paris," he said.

And then he placed his hands on his ears and removed a mask from his face. I was astonished and frozen there because I saw fisher standing with a mask in his hand."

"You helped me to get away from his clutches and told me to lead a peaceful life. So it was my turn to help you."

"So there you go, Fisher fooled you."

"You brat, how could you do this to me."

And suddenly, there were heavy footsteps being heard and a gun battle was heard. Manuel got tense and turned his eyes towards the door. Taking the opportunity, Jimmy stood up and banged the chair on Manuel.

The chair broke into pieces with the arm piece in his hand. Manuel fell to the ground unconscious. Catherine too did the same thing and with only two pieces of wood they beat up all the men.

Then a big sound was heard as the policemen arrived. By breaking the door, they quickly caught hold of Manuel. He was still unconscious, but was enough for him to land behind bars.

Jimmy and Catherine hugged together and were happy about the end of the mission.

Inspector Rout came inside with a big smile.

"Thanks Jimmy, for catching the drug lord. We had been trying to nab them since you went to Jail. The police dept. will be grateful to you."

"Enough of praises Rout, now we are in a hurry, sorry for that."

♪ ♪ ♪

Back at the HQ, Jimmy and Catherine were dressed in formals. Just as they were entering the room, Jimmy stopped wondering if he had forgotten something. After a detailed check of his pockets and dress, he moved inside the room and stood beside Catherine near Mr. A's table which was placed at the centre of the office room.

"Welcome back agents. After four months of investigation, you have solved the case. Congratulations."

"What about Manuel?" asked Catherine?

"Well, he is facing smuggling and criminal charges from both France and India. Now it's up to Govt. to decide where his trial will be held."

"Sir, I just have one request," Jimmy said leaning forward.

"Yes, go on what I can do for you."

"Sir, I just want you to make sure Fisher is safe."

"Okay agent, we will make sure that he is safe."

The conversation went on for a few minutes. Mr. A kept answering all the queries about Manuel and his team. Suddenly in the middle, Mr. A interrupted the conversation and said, "Jimmy, I want you to know that you two have to solve one more case then I think, I will consider your promotion."

And why is it like that?" Catherine asked,

"Rules and regulations have to go according to it," Mr. A replied back. Oh! I forgot something; I have a surprise for you."

The door of the room opened and a tall man entered the room. He was wearing a grey over coat with a stylish cap. He gave a smile to Jimmy and Catherine as they recognised him.

"Agents, meet our new recruit, agent Fisher."

Jimmy and Catherine were astonished and surprised to see him.

"Agent Fisher reporting sir," Fisher said, saluting Mr .A tapping his legs.

"Have a seat," Mr. A said.

"Jimmy, you told me to keep him safe. There he is safe now."

"Thank you, sir. Any details about our next mission?"

"Not now Jimmy. Cases have not popped up. When we have something, I will let you know."

They all thanked Mr. A and bid farewell to him. Jimmy was thinking about a party, when Mr. A stopped him.

"Wait, you guys meet me at the Silent restaurant at 8 p.m. sharp.

"Yes sir, you got it," Jimmy replied.

8 p.m. sharp at the restaurant. The three agents arrived. They spotted Mr. A holding the menu card.

"Sir, why have you called us here?" Fisher asked.

"Yes, have a seat."

After seated comfortably, the waiter poured water in the glass and Mr. A held his glass in the air. "A toast to our victory."

After cheers, Mr. A called out Jimmy and said, "Jimmy and Catherine, I will be glad to hear the story of your first Adventure."

"Sir…… I will be glad to narrate it to you," Catherine said.

"It all started nine years ago on a beautiful fine morning……….

Acknowledgement

I sincerely thank my dearest mother whose constant motivation and guidance has resulted in the publishing of my first book. My father, who took time from his tight schedule, to type my novel. English teachers at my school who kept helping me with my sentence formations and my grammatical errors and lastly my best buddies at school who kept telling me that I could do it.